Haunting GHOST

USA TODAY BESTELLING AUTHOR

KRISTINE ALLEN

People used to know me as Lucian Stone. I'm a cleaner for the Ankeny RBMC. Some would call me heartless; others might say I'm emotionless. They might be right, but I have two fingers for them.

When I was young and thought I had the world by the tail, Lila Kellerman owned my heart.

Once upon a time we'd been that couple—the epitome of young love. Voted most likely to succeed. Cutest couple. Quintessential small-town-jock meets blonde girl-next-door. Until one night it all went to shit.

At eighteen and two months shy of graduating, the clang of iron bars closing became my background music.

Gone were the boy with a full-ride scholarship for football and the girl with hopes of becoming a veterinarian. In their place were an ex-con and a dead girl.

My name is Ghost, and this is my story.

Featured characters:

Griz and unnamed members from the Savanah RBMC Chapter by Erin Trejo

Creed, Reaper, Winchester, and Justice from the Jacksonville RBMC Chapter by Kathleen Kelly

To Rhiannon... there is no measure for my gratitude because there could never be enough.

PROLOGUE

Lucian

I'd had a crush on Lila Kellerman since fourth grade—except I never realized it at the time. I was just a kid. She was in second grade, and her class came out to the playground when mine did.

I'll never forget the day I noticed her. My friends and I were tossing a football to each other in a big circle, and she was jumping rope with some other little girls. She was wearing a frilly pink dress, which was weird because the rest of the girls were wearing jeans and T-shirts. Her sunshine-yellow hair was in pigtails, and they bounced as she jumped over the rope with each swing.

"Who's that?" I asked Teddy, my best friend, as I spun the ball in my hand.

He glanced over his shoulder to the group of girls. Then he shrugged. "New girl that moved here from Charleston. Lily, or Libby. Something like that."

"Huh," I said as I watched them jump and laugh. "Why she wearing that frou-frou dress?"

"I don't know," he said in exasperation. "Throw the dang ball!"

Teddy thought he was so tough by saying "dang."

Irritated at him for no specific reason I could name, I threw the ball at him. It hit him in the chest so hard, he fell to his ass in the dirt.

"Geez, Lucian! Easy!"

His complaint fell on deaf ears, because I was walking over to the girl in the pink dress like something had control of my feet. When I got closer, it was like I was being pulled into her orbit like a tractor beam on *Star Trek* or something. She was magnetic.

"Who are you?" she asked as she stopped jumping and cocked her head at me.

I'd never seen eyes so crystal blue in all my life. All ten years of it. For a moment I was tongue-tied, and all I could do was stare at her.

"Are you deaf?" she asked me with a worried frown as she stepped closer. I continued to blink at her like an idiot. Until she took my hand and little sparks went up my arm like when you hold a sparkler too close to the lit end. "It's okay if you are. We can still be friends."

The giggles of the other girls shook me out of my daze, and my brows dropped into a frown. "I ain't deaf. I just never seen you here before. What's your name?"

She gave me a haughty little huff. "I asked you first."

I grinned at her spunk. "My name's Lucian. I'm in fourth grade."

"Well, Lucian-in-fourth-grade, I'm Lila." She paused before she leaned closer like she was gonna tell me a secret. Then she whispered, "In second grade."

A stupid smile spread so far, my cheeks hurt. "Like the Eric Clapton song?"

"The who?" she asked, and her face wrinkled up in confusion.

"Layla," I clarified but shook my head. I had no idea why I expected her to know who Eric Clapton was when none of my friends did. He was my dad's favorite singer.

"Ohhh. No, Lila," she said with a smile.

"Okay, um, never mind," I mumbled.

Before I could ask her anything else, the recess teacher blew the whistle, and we all needed to line up to go back inside.

"You wasted the last five minutes of recess talking to that weird girl," Teddy complained. "We could've been throwing the football all that time."

I glared at him, and he immediately shut his mouth.

As we filed inside, I glanced over to see Lila lined up with her class, waiting to go in. She gave me a bright dimpled smile and waved. My heart went all funny, and I ducked my head to hide the smile that wouldn't go away.

Lila and I became best friends, but I'd never tell Teddy, Mike, Jerry, or Todd that. They wouldn't understand. Turned out, she lived in the neighborhood two blocks behind my house. Her neighborhood was new, and my mom said that's where all the "hoity-toity" people lived.

She had a swing set that, no shit, looked like a freaking castle—complete with a drawbridge. It was the coolest thing I'd ever seen.

On the nights that my mom left for the bar well before dinner, I would traipse down to her neighborhood and sit on her swing set. She would bring out a plate of food to me, and we would sit in the castle part while I ate.

I knew her mom made the plates up, because I caught her looking out through the curtains sometimes.

"How come your dad is always gone?" she asked me one night as she leaned against the wall of the castle as I ate. Her skinny arms were looped around her knees. One had a Band-Aid on it with colored stars.

Not making eye contact, I shrugged as I shoveled a huge bite of potatoes in my mouth. I was super hungry because it was Saturday and Mom had slept late that morning, so all I had for breakfast was a bowl of dry cereal because we had no milk. For lunch, I had a sandwich from the deli down the street, because she gave me five bucks when she left for bingo. But I'd been playing football with the boys all afternoon, and that sandwich had worn off quick.

"He works on the road a lot. He does construction stuff," I replied.

"Why doesn't your mom cook?" she asked.

"She never learned how, I guess," I said with a shrug. In my eleven years, I'd never known my mom to cook a thing. When Dad was home, he cooked, but that wasn't very often. Usually, I had a frozen dinner unless Mom gave me money to go down to the little deli for a sandwich.

"Hmm," she hummed. Then she was quiet until I finished eating.

"How many stars do you think are up there?" I asked her. We were lying on the cool grass. I'd turned twelve that day, but no one knew.

Funny thing was, I didn't feel any different than when I was eleven. I never understood birthdays.

"Gazillions." She sighed happily as she rested her folded hands over her stomach.

I snorted. "There's no such thing as gazillions," I said. Her head rolled in my direction, and she shot me a glare.

"Is so."

"Is not."

"Is so!"

"Not," I teased, suppressing a grin. For a smiley, sweet thing, she was so easy to rile up sometimes.

"Lucian Donovan Stone, you don't know! You're only saying that because you can't count that high!" Her nose wrinkled as she continued to glare, and I couldn't help it. I busted out laughing.

"Like you can?" I retorted between laughs as I wiped the tears from my eyes.

"Why do you like making me mad?" she asked before she poked my arm.

I rolled to my side and propped my head on the heel of my hand.

"Because you're always so perfect and sweet. I gotta make sure you're real sometimes."

She rolled her eyes. "I don't know why I'm friends with you," she said with a huff.

"Because you like being friends with the coolest guy in school?" I teased.

"You're so full of yourself," she said, but I saw her lips twitch, telling me she wanted to laugh. She went back to looking at the tiny specks of light that twinkled in the dark night sky.

"Lila?" I asked as I reached out to touch the ends of her golden hair that was splayed across the grass.

"Yeah?"

"Are we always gonna be friends?" I asked. I was afraid to lose her friendship and her family that seemed to care about me more than my own. She rolled her head in my direction again and gave me a huge smile.

"Duh. Of course. Until all the stars fall from the sky," she said.

"Lucian?"

"Yeah?" I asked as I threw the football to her. She was a lousy catcher, and it sailed right through her hands. Totally undeterred, she ran after it, then ran back before she tossed it underhand to me. I grinned but didn't say anything. I'd tried a million times to teach her the proper way to throw a football, but she never got it.

"When is your birthday?"

"Huh?" I asked as I held the slightly flat and fraying ball poised to throw. I'd played with it for so long, the laces were starting to come undone. It had been my pride and joy since I found it in the neighbors' trash when they moved out three years ago.

"You come to my house all the time, but I never go to yours. And you come to my birthday party every year, but I never go to yours. I thought we were best friends, but you never invite me to your party. Does your family not believe in parties?" She crossed her arms and tried to look mad, but I could see the hurt in her eyes.

My face burned, and I stubbed my scuffed shoe in the grass. "It's not that they don't believe in parties. My family, uh, we don't celebrate birthdays," I said. It wasn't really a lie. We didn't. But neither did my mom so much as tell me happy thirteenth birthday.

"Well, I'm making a new rule."

"Oh yeah? What's that?" I asked, not making eye contact and twirling the ball as I tossed it up in the air. I cast an occasional glance her way as I did.

"I'm having a birthday party for you this year," she said with a decisive nod.

"You can't," I said with a smirk.

"Why not?"

"Because it's already passed," I said with a shrug.

"Then next year," she insisted.

"Sure." I grinned and tossed the ball to her. That time, she surprised the hell outta me, because she caught it like a pro. Her eyes popped wide, and I knew it had surprised her too.

"When is it?" she asked.

A sigh left my lips as I rolled my eyes. "Anyone ever tell you you're like a little bulldog?"

Her fists hit her hips, and her bony elbows stuck out on either side.

"That's not nice. When is your birthday?"

"It's November seventeenth," I finally admitted.

"That was last week!" she shouted, appalled.

I shrugged. The next day, her mom made me a birthday cake, complete with candles and a gift. It was a new football with my own air pump for it.

"Happy birthday to you," Lila, her parents, and my friends finished singing to me, and I blew out the candles.

I hadn't bothered telling my mom they were throwing me a party, because she always talked shit about them when she knew I'd been hanging out there. I'd taken to sneaking out to go over when she was home. Most of the time I didn't need to, because she was never there.

"You're so lucky the Kellermans spoil you," Teddy said as he walked home with me. He was going to spend the night, because he had stolen a bottle of booze from his parents. He said it was for us to celebrate me turning fourteen. He wouldn't be fourteen until May.

Watching the ground as we crossed the field, I shrugged. "They're nice people," I said.

"They're loaded," he said with a snicker.

"It's not about that," I argued.

"Whatever." He was done with the conversation.

We entered my quiet, empty house. Teddy thought it was cool that I got to have the house to myself so much. In all honesty, it sucked.

Again, there had been no birthday wishes from my mom before she left. I got a "do the dishes and make sure the house is clean. I don't want to come home to a shithole" as she lit a cigarette and looked down her nose at me. Same old, same old.

The only thing different about that year was that my dad gave me a gift before he left to go out of town that morning. It was a yellow pocketknife, and I almost cried. It was the first gift I could remember getting from him. "You're fourteen now. That makes you a man. Every man needs a knife."

I had no idea why he thought fourteen made me a man, but I wasn't gonna argue.

"Thanks, Dad," I said as I held it reverently in my palm. He ruffled my hair and left.

That night, Teddy and I drank vodka until we puked.

My dad never came home again.

The summer after I turned fifteen was utterly miserable. Lila was different.

First of all, she had *boobs*. And my dick acted weird around her. I hated that. She was my best friend, not some chick. Chicks were different than Lila. Lila was special.

Chicks had started falling all over me at the start of last year. It was weird, but I wasn't complaining. I'd been getting blowjobs since I was thirteen, but I never told her that. The cashier at the grocery store had taken my virginity at the beginning of the summer, and I thought I was hot shit because she was seventeen.

Lila was on a pedestal. If any guy tried to get her to do those things to him, I'd blacken his eye.

Yet, I couldn't deny that she had been my person for over five years. That didn't mean I should be looking at her like *that*.

The other thing was, she and her friends started spending more time together, and she had less time for me. I hated that too.

When she stayed with her friends, I made sure to spend the night with one of the guys to keep my mind off it. On the nights she was home, we snuck out to the gazebo that had replaced her swing set.

We were all at the lake, and I was trying not to make it obvious that I was looking at her as she laughed with her friends while they lay out in their bikinis. I'd convinced the guys to stand in the water to throw the football because I had a fucking boner.

A boner.

From looking at Lila.

I was going to hell.

"Goddamn, have you noticed that Lila has great tits already?" Mike asked. My eyes narrowed, and I threw the football at his head as he ogled Lila. It knocked him over, and he fell back under the water. We all laughed.

"Hey!" he shouted after he came up above the water, sputtering.

"Quit looking at Lila's tits," I grumbled. "That's fucked-up."

"Yeah. Those are Lucian's tits," Teddy said with a snort of laughter.

"Fuck you. She's my friend," I insisted.

"Oh yeah?" Jerry asked with a smirk as he caught the ball from Mike.

"Yeah," I ground out.

"Huh. Then you wouldn't care if I asked her out?" Jerry said with a leer as he threw the ball to Todd.

"She's only thirteen. Leave her alone." My anger was growing, and I was two seconds away from kicking my friend's ass.

"Yeah, she belongs to Lucian. Always has and always will," Todd quietly murmured. He never spoke a lot, so we all swiveled our heads to look at him. He shrugged. "What? It's true."

"Whatever," I muttered as I caught the ball he threw.

The year I turned sixteen, I couldn't stand it anymore. I asked Lila to be my girl.

She said yes.

PART I

ONE

Lucian

"LAYLA"—ERIC CLAPTON

Eric Clapton's "Layla" was playing softly on my MP3 player that was plugged in next to the bed. I was singing softly and changing each "Layla" to "Lila," making her smile. It was my favorite song, and I did that every time it played.

"Please don't do anything stupid," Lila said as she rested her chin on her hands over my heart that beat for her. We were lying on the mattress and box spring I had on the floor in my room.

My arm tightened around her waist as I grinned. "Never. I have too much to lose, baby."

Not only did I have my full-ride scholarship to Clemson, I had her. Truth be told, she was more important to me than any scholarship. My fingers twirled her golden hair. She was the best thing that had ever happened to me, and I couldn't believe I was lucky enough to call her my girl.

"I wish I hadn't said I'd babysit for the Millers tonight. I'd go with you," she said with a pout. I grabbed her ass and pulled her up to straddle me. Her tank top did nothing to hide her nipples that hardened as I bit my lip and lifted my hips up to grind on her.

"Again?" she asked with a chuckle. She'd given me her virginity on her sixteenth birthday last month—I cherished it and her.

"We have forty-five minutes before you have to leave. Let's make it count," I offered with a smirk before I rolled us over and we went one more round.

By the time we were pulling our clothes on, we were sweaty and slightly breathless. The afternoon sunlight shone through the holes of the afghan I had nailed up over my window. It sprinkled drops of sun on her face and shoulders.

I paused and stroked my thumb over the curve of her cheek. "You are beautiful, Lila Marie Kellerman," I murmured. She gave me a soft smile that sent my heart thumping and my gut fluttering like a fucking girl.

"So are you, Lucian Donovan Stone."

I laughed at her. I wasn't beautiful, but somehow I got lucky enough that she thought so, and that was enough for me.

"Are you always gonna be my girl?"

"Until all the stars fall from the sky. Duh," she said as she kissed the inside of my wrist.

"Good, because I'll always be your man. Never forget that while I'm gone next year." The thought of leaving her for college tore my insides up, but it was a means to an end. I was good, and I knew it. If I could keep from getting hurt, my goal was to get drafted into the NFL. Then I'd be able to give her all the things she deserved.

"Never. My heart could never belong to anyone but you."

She was everything good and pure in the world. The

brightest smile always paired with laughing blue eyes the color of a cloudless summer sky. Hair the color of sunshine and golden wheat, skin alabaster and moonlight.

But it wasn't only her exterior beauty that set her apart.

Inside she was the brightest star, a butterfly unfurling its wings for the first time, the scent of springtime, and glittering raindrops on the tips of a rose. No idea how I'd won her over, but we were the epitome of young love—all soft smiles and gentle touches.

Fuck, she made me feel all kinds of weird shit.

She stretched up on her tiptoes and pressed her perfect pink lips to mine.

Fuck, I'd happily climb back in that bed with her if we could.

"Always and forever, baby," I said before I nipped her lip and held her close.

))

The boys and I had been at the party out by the lake, but when a few older guys showed up that seemed like trouble, I said I was leaving. They pulled out a shit-ton of weed and started trying to sell it to people. I was out. I'd only had a couple of beers, and I knew I was okay to drive.

"Dude, don't be a party pooper," Teddy said as he stood in front of me. Jerry, Mike, and Todd flanked him as they waited to see what panned out. I was their ride, so if I left, they were stuck there until someone sobered up. Either that, or they left with me.

"If you wanna stay, then stay. Not only am I eighteen, I'm not doing anything to risk my scholarship." God knew, my mom wouldn't pay for my college if I messed up by doing something stupid. That was if she could afford it to begin with.

He huffed, then glanced around as he decided what to do.

"Fine, then how about if we take the party to your house? Your mom probably isn't home, right?"

Of course she wasn't. My dad was out of the picture, and Mom would likely be closing down the bar.

"Yeah, that's fine," I mumbled. Kip and Hank came sauntering up as I was pulling out my keys.

"Where you guys going?" Kip asked.

"We're taking the party to Lucian's," Teddy said. I punched him in the arm. "Ow, why'd you do that?"

I didn't want a bunch of people hanging out at the house. Us five was one thing, because they knew what my house was like. I didn't invite a lot of people over, because it was embarrassing. Kip was my friend, but his family had money and a nice house. Hank, I didn't know all that well.

"Hey, let us bum a ride. I can't drive, and he certainly isn't in any shape to drive either," Kip said as he thumbed over his shoulder at Hank who was swaying slightly as he stood there.

"I have my truck. We won't all fit," I said. I'd bought the fifteen-year-old truck with money I'd scraped together from doing lawn work and odd jobs around football practice. It wasn't fancy, but it was solid and it ran.

"We'll ride in the back," Kip said.

Blowing out a frustrated sigh of resignation, I nodded. "Get in."

Todd, Mike, and Jerry piled in the extended cab, Teddy got in the passenger seat, and Kip climbed in the bed with Hank. We were going down the dirt road flanked by trees with Hank Williams blaring from the speakers and the windows down.

I heard the crack of a can being opened, and I glanced in the rearview to see Mike taking a drink of a beer.

"What the fuck are you doing?" I reached back and snagged it from him. Some of it spilled in my lap, and I threw it angrily out the window. "You got more of that?" I demanded as I looked at him in the rearview.

He sullenly shook his head. Jerry smacked him on the back of his shaggy mop of hair.

"Dumbass," Jerry muttered.

"That was alcohol abuse!" Kip yelled through the open slider in the back window.

"Shut up," I hollered as I glanced back at him.

When my eyes hit the road, I panicked. Two deer had jumped out of the trees, and I tried to swerve to miss them. I clipped one and overcorrected. My tires caught the loose edge of the road, and I lost control.

Everything seemed to happen in slow motion.

The truck fishtailed before sliding. The ass-end came around until we were perpendicular with the road, and then we were rolling.

During one of the flips, my head hit the frame around the window, and I blacked out.

When I came to, there were flashing lights everywhere and more people than I knew existed out there. I tried to look around to see where the rest of the guys were, but my chest screamed in agony, and a plastic-and-foam collar was around my neck. Something warm was running down my face.

"Fuck," I muttered as I tried to sit up but was quickly pushed back down. I hurt so goddamn bad.

"Son, don't move. You're in bad shape, and you might have fractured your neck," a paramedic said to me as he shined a light in my eyes and started asking me a million questions. Then they prepared to load me up.

"What happened? Where is everyone?" I asked, confused as hell and feeling nauseous.

The paramedics glanced at each other but didn't answer me.

As I was being lifted into the back of one of the ambulances, I saw a long black bag sitting on another stretcher. Horror filled me, and I prayed that I'd wake up from the nightmare I was stuck in.

On the way to the hospital, I died three times.

Crazy, huh?

TWO

Lila

"GONE (.GRAV3S VERSION)"—RED

My junior year was the year of Lucian's trial.

"Lucian, I begged my dad to help, but he said he couldn't because of his position. As it is, he couldn't or wouldn't prosecute the case because of your close connection with our family. I guess the assistant DA and Dad don't get along really well. Dad is afraid he's gunning for you because he knows Dad likes you." I held Lucian's hand as we rested in the grass much as we did when we were little.

He sighed as he stared up at the stars.

"I'm sure he knows your dad paid my bail," Lucian murmured.

It went without saying that it didn't help that we lived in a small community and everyone knew everyone. Lucian might've been the town football hero, but he wasn't from the "right crowd."

"You have a bright future. It was an accident, Lucian. The

judge is going to see that," I said as I squeezed his hand and curled into his side.

I was wrong.

Lucian was charged with vehicular manslaughter, and the prosecutor pushed the fact that he was drinking underage. It was an absolute shitshow of a trial. It dragged on and on—painfully so. All because Kip had a rich daddy and Lucian was from the wrong side of the tracks.

Lucian had a public defender, and the guy was a douche.

"Lucian, you have too much against you. The Harpers have a lot of money and influence. They're pushing for the max punishment. If you're willing to take a deal, I think I can get you five years—out in less, if you're lucky," the dumbass said.

"That's ridiculous," my father barked. "We can fight this. They are blowing everything out of proportion on this. Anyone can see that. Lucian is a good kid. No history of trouble. Football scholarship. He has a future. Any deal they'd be willing to toss his way since the trial already started would be absolute dog shit."

"There's a real chance they could throw the book at him too," Ralph Rutherford III argued. A douchey name for a big, fat douche. I hated him and I wished Lucian would've let us help hire an attorney, but he was embarrassed that my dad had already paid his bail.

When I saw the defeat in Lucian's eyes, I knew he was giving up.

"Don't do this, Lucian," I begged. He dropped his gaze to his clasped hands, and I wanted to scream.

The rest was a blur.

The day of his sentencing, he tried to convince me not to go. Maybe it would've been better if I hadn't. When they read the results of his ridiculous plea bargain, I burst into tears and leaned over the rail to hug him, but was pulled away when the bailiff stepped in. The judge demanded attention, and his words were nothing but a droning buzz.

Lucian cast one last glance my way before he swallowed hard and dropped his gaze. As they led him away, he wouldn't make eye contact, and I knew in my heart he was shutting down.

"Dad," I cried into my father's chest as he and my mom held me. The tension in his body bespoke his anger. My parents loved Lucian. Now he was being taken away from us.

He went to prison with a five-year sentence.

I immediately wrote to him. His first letter to me was like razor blades to my soul.

The day I got that letter, I thought someone had shot the sun from the sky. In the words that blurred as I tried to read, he told me he didn't want to hear from me again, and my heart shattered. Sure, he sugarcoated his request with bullshit like he didn't want me wasting my life waiting, and I deserved better. Blah, blah, blah.

I didn't listen. I wrote. Letter after letter. They all came back. He refused them. If my heart hadn't been obliterated before, it certainly was after that.

At first I wanted to crumple to the floor and wallow in the loss of the boy who I'd foolishly thought would be my forever. Then I picked myself up and stitched my heart back together. The problem with mending a broken heart is it's never the same after that. None of the pieces fit properly anymore.

"Hey, you going to Kevin's party this weekend?" my friend Noelle asked as I swapped out books from my locker then zipped my backpack up. I closed the door with a clang to see her leaning against the locker next to mine, holding her books to her chest. Her red hair was pulled up in a high, bouncy ponytail, and her green eyes sparkled at the thought of the pending weekend.

I shrugged. "I'm not sure yet," I said as I gave her a smile that barely lifted the corners of my mouth. After slinging my backpack over my shoulder, I twisted my hair up and shoved a pen through it.

Her shoulders fell. "Lila, you need to let it go. He's gone. He made it very clear he wants you to live your life. Are you going to wait five years to see if *maybe* he will talk to you when he gets out of prison?"

Though she spoke the truth, it hurt. I couldn't believe it had been nearly a year since Lucian had gone to prison. I was getting ready to graduate. He was supposed to be there for my ceremony. Then I'd go to Clemson so we could be together. That's how things were supposed to go. Now they never would.

I knew everyone was looking forward to the party. Everyone but me, that was. Summer's heat was already in full humid effect, and everyone was restless to be done with high school. It would be our last summer together before we all went our separate ways in life.

"That's not fair," I said, fighting off the burning in my eyes and the hollow feeling in my chest.

"Life's not fair. But you need to keep living it." Her gaze pleaded with me, but I hardened my heart.

"I'll think about it," I finally said as I brushed past her to get to my last class of the day.

The party was being held out by Kevin's grandparents' house, down by the pond. They had agreed to it as long as no one left. The shadow of what had happened with Lucian and the boys two years ago was still heavy over our community.

Though I really didn't want to, my dad actually was the one to encourage me to go. He'd smiled and said, "You're eighteen now. You'll be leaving for college, and it will be time to bury your nose in the books. I trust you, and you deserve to go have some fun. Just call me if you drink and don't want to stay, and I'll pick you up."

At first I was shocked. His younger sister Priscilla had died before I was born when she was hit by a drunk driver. That was why I initially thought my dad would never believe Lucian was innocent—because alcohol had been involved. Yet he had surprised me and had faith in Lucian.

In the end, I decided maybe he was right, and I broke down and went.

Music blared from a speaker set up in the back of someone's truck, and laughter rang out around us. Teddy sat next to me and looped an arm around my shoulders as he leaned in to whisper in my ear, "Hey, Lila, you wanna go to the back of my truck to look at the stars?"

With a sigh, I shrugged his arm off me. "No. I'm fine here. Thanks."

He scoffed, and the beer on his breath made me want to gag. "We all know you were fucking Lucian every chance you had. Don't act like you're all virginal, Lila."

My mouth fell open, and the tears that had been burning in my eyes since my conversation with Noelle blurred my vision. I stood and started to stalk to my car.

"Lila, wait! I'm sorry," he said as he came after me and grabbed my arm. I threw my bottle of Diet Coke at him.

"Fuck you, Teddy. You were supposed to be his friend—*my* friend. Let go of me." I shook my arm, and he let go. Regret was in his eyes, but I didn't care. I was done.

Ignoring the glances I got from the partygoers as I passed, I stormed across the field to where my car was parked with the rest along the private dirt road. Feet pounding behind me had me pausing.

"Lila! Where are you going? We're not supposed to leave," Noelle said with her brow furrowed, panting from her run to catch up to me.

"I haven't had a drop to drink unless you count Diet Coke. I'm going home."

"Lila, please—" she began, but I cut her off.

"You go have fun. I'll see you Monday."

She sighed, and defeat was etched on her face as I climbed in my car and backed out. When I reached the main driveway, Kevin's grandfather was set up as a sentinel.

"Great," I muttered as I rolled down my window.

"Lila, girl. You know I said no one was to leave." His shaggy brows lowered as he spoke.

"I know, Mr. Brenager. But I swear, I haven't had a drop of alcohol. Wanna smell my breath?" I asked with a grin that I hoped seemed brighter than I felt.

"Yes," he said as he crossed his arms over his chest. "And get out. I wanna see you do that sobriety stuff."

Jesus. "Okay?" I put my car in park, got out, blew in his face, walked heel to toe, touched my nose and any other thing I could think of before he finally huffed.

"Fine. But anything happens and it will be on your conscience," he grumbled. I thought I heard him mumble something about a kid my age not needing a car like I had too. Inside I was rolling my eyes. My dad was the district attorney and had done well for himself in private practice before that. They were older when I was born, and they tended to spoil me. The Mercedes was an early graduation present.

"Yes, sir," I said as he let me get back in my car and pull out of the gate. The night was pitch-black out on the country road, and I gripped the wheel tightly with clammy hands. I didn't breathe easy until I was on the blacktop and headed back to town.

The entire way home, I thought about Lucian. I missed him so much, my chest ached every damn day.

When I pulled in the driveway, I was relieved to see the lights on. My parents were supportive and the best parents anyone could ask for. My dad had taught me that hard work got you the nicer things in life. While he may have bought me the car, it was only because I'd maintained straight As despite what had happened. Little did he know, I'd poured myself into my studies so I didn't have as much time to think.

I let myself in and shuffled to the family room where the TV was on. "Hey, Mom. Dad. I decided to come home early."

No one answered. Confusion marred my brow as I glanced around.

Where are they?

"Dad! Mom!" I called out. I heard a noise in my dad's home office and assumed they were in there, so I went around the large sectional and froze. Shock hit me, and I began to tremble violently.

My parents were slumped over on the couch. My dad still had his arms around my mom, and their eyes stared vacantly. Blood was everywhere.

I began to hyperventilate, then I fumbled for my phone to call 911. A crashing sound in the office had me dropping the phone as my heart raced.

Two men came out of the office with a box stuffed full of files and my dad's laptop. Their eyes were hard and cold as they stared at me. They seemed familiar, but I had no clue who they were. One had greased-back black hair. The other had shaggy red hair and a scraggly beard.

Then another man sauntered through the door like he had no cares in the world. That man, I recognized immediately. Luis

Trujillo was the head of one of the biggest cartel families in the world. The man was known for his ruthlessness. It shocked me to see him in my home. Who were we to him?

The first man leered before the second raised his hand.

The sound seemed to register after the ripping burn in my chest stole my ability to breathe. Boneless, I crumpled to the floor. Unable to bring air in, blackness crept in from the edges of my vision.

Feet stopped in front of me, but I couldn't raise my gaze.

"I can't believe you shot her, you stupid fucking idiot," one said.

"She saw us!" the other argued.

"We're done here. Let's go," Luis said as he stepped over me like I was trash at his feet.

Cold trickled up my limbs, and darkness closed in further. "We could've made a lot off her! What a waste."

Another blast hit me, and the abyss swallowed me.

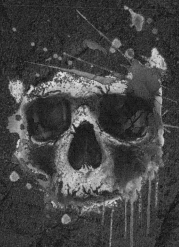

THREE

Lucian

"INVISIBLE MAN"—THEORY OF A DEADMAN

Footsteps echoed down the hall as I ducked into the bathroom. As quietly as I could, I closed the door and climbed on the toilet. Crouched down, I knew it was a shitty hiding place. The doors were short and didn't lock. My heart was pounding so hard, I was afraid they'd hear it.

The ridiculous hiding place wouldn't protect me for long if they looked under or busted the door in, but I was only hoping to buy time until a guard came along. The bathrooms weren't really made to keep anyone out. It was a prison, for fuck's sake.

"Where did he go?" a raspy voice asked. There were several murmured replies, but I was too busy holding my breath and praying.

One by one, the doors were ripped open. The partitions shook with the force of the wood banging on the opposite side.

Eyes squeezed shut, I wished I could disappear. It had been nearly a year, and I'd been dodging the fuckers the entire time. Evidently, my time had run out. How they made it into the character-based housing was beyond me. They were assholes.

BANG! My door crashed, and my eyes popped open as I prepared to fight.

"What the fuck?"

"Where did he go?"

"He had to have come in here. There's nowhere else he could've gone," the last one said.

Confusion hit me, but I kept my mouth shut as I looked around. They were looking right at me. I glanced down and saw the same orange prison garb I wore every day.

They checked each stall again as I watched Faulkner crouch down to watch the floor.

"He didn't go under the stalls. I don't know how, but he's not here," he said as he stood up.

They looked up at the ceiling as if I'd be hanging out up there like Spider-Man.

Finally, the three of them left, muttering.

I looked down at myself again, held my hand up, and stared at it front and back. What the fuck? Were they blind?

"You can come out now," a gruff voice said, and I looked up in surprise. Wrapped up in my shock, I hadn't heard anyone else come in.

It was one of the older inmates, Dennison. Despite being my bunkmate, he kept to himself. Rumor was, he was in some motorcycle gang out of Savannah. He also worked in the garage with me, but we hadn't really interacted much. I'd been fortunate to snag the position, because it would give me something to do when I got out. It showed that I was trustworthy too. An inmate had to be if they were allowed to work in the shop.

"You deaf, kid? I said you were safe. You don't need to hide anymore." His words momentarily dragged me back to the day I'd met Lila.

Cautiously, I climbed down off the toilet and stepped out into the open bathroom.

"Why are you on my side?" I asked as I tried to slow down my breathing and heart rate.

The only sign that I startled him was a slight tensing in his jaw and his eyes darting around.

"Where are you? You do that often, and you're going to get way more attention than you bargained for," he said as he leaned back on a sink and lit a joint. Something we definitely weren't supposed to have. He tucked the lighter in his shoe.

I was standing right in front of him, but he seemed to look through me. I waved my hand in his face, and he didn't so much as flinch. To say I was shocked would be an understatement.

Then I began to worry. What the fuck was going on? Had I suddenly become the invisible man? Jesus, what if this was me for the rest of my fucking life? I needed him to see me!

"There you are!" he said, and I stared at him. He chuckled, and I glanced down to see I still looked the same.

"What the fuck is happening?" I asked.

He tipped his head back slightly and took a deep drag as he looked down his nose at me.

"Now that, I can't say. What I do think is when you get out of here, there are some people I know that you should meet," he said after he blew the smoke to the ceiling.

"We're not supposed to have drugs," I muttered, causing him to laugh.

"Son, do you do everything you're told?"

"I mean…." I trailed off, not knowing how to answer that. I

was no angel, but I wouldn't say I was a bad person. No matter the fact I was sitting in a South Carolina prison.

"Yeah, that's what I thought."

"Well, how can I meet people you know when we aren't supposed to hang out and shit after we get out of here?" I stubbornly asked.

"You ain't gonna be on parole forever. Besides, it's not me that you'd be hanging out with. It would be my brother and his chapter." He stubbed out the joint and waited for it to cool before tucking it in a tiny tear in his clothes.

"Okay?" I frowned in confusion.

"Call me Griz," he said as he gripped my shoulder and looked me in the eye.

"Griz," I repeated.

"Stick with me, kid. I'll make sure those assholes know you're with me, and if they fuck with you they'll be dealing with every chapter of the Royal Bastards in the country."

That was the first time I found out I had a gift. If you could call it that. I had no idea what the fuck it was or why it happened to me. It freaked me the fuck out.

Two days later, I was walking into the shop for work as part of the prison rehabilitation programs. One of the guards was reading the paper, and I happened to see the front-page headline when he set it down to watch me come in. It had me stopping in my tracks.

"Sir?"

The guard frowned. "What?"

"Would you mind?" I asked, gesturing to the paper, telling myself there was no way I'd seen what I thought. "I only wanted to get a better look at the article on the front page."

"The murder? Sick fucker there. Whoever did it better hope they don't end up here," he said as he handed it over with a shake of his head. "Who kills an entire family like that? A teenage girl, to boot. Such a waste."

Hands shaking, I scanned the printed words, and my heart stopped. Literally stopped beating for a good minute. I couldn't breathe. My stomach revolted, and I rushed to the trash can and lost my breakfast.

"Damn, kid, you okay?" The guard was watching me with wide eyes. "Do you need to go to the infirmary?"

Shaking my head, I fought tears that would likely get my ass beat if it got out. My head hung. Then I croaked, "That was my girl."

"Jesus, Stone. I'm sorry."

Griz glanced at me as he passed but didn't stop because it wouldn't be tolerated for him to socialize when he was supposed to be working.

"You okay to work? I can take you to the infirmary if you need me to," the guard said quietly.

Not wanting to get him in trouble when there wasn't anything physically wrong with me, I shook my head. Then I shoved my grief down deep to deal with later.

All day I worked like a man possessed, not stopping for lunch. When it was quitting time, one of the guards took us to chow, which I didn't eat. Then we were returned to our bay. No one spoke to me all day. It didn't take long for word to travel in prison.

I didn't give the guards any trouble. I did as I was told; I didn't question; I didn't fight. A few watched over me because they saw their own kids in me. I knew it, they knew it, but no one said anything aloud. Maybe that's why even the usually dickish guards treated me like a human that day.

After lights out, as I lay in my bed staring at the bunk above me, silent tears slipped from the corners of my eyes. Though I wanted to scream, I didn't dare.

"Kid? You all right?" Griz asked quietly from the top bunk.

"Yeah," I choked out, wincing at the crack in my voice.

He sighed, and I knew he didn't believe me but was granting me my privacy to grieve.

What felt like razor blades shredded my insides. Grief destroyed what heart I had left. The boy that was Lucian Donovan Stone died that day.

I'd made peace with the path my life had taken because I told myself Lila would live a good life full of happiness. Now? Nothing seemed to matter.

There would never be another woman for me as long as I lived. As I did each night, I hated that I couldn't see the stars. Because that night, I knew they were all falling from the sky.

That night, I truly became a ghost.

FOUR

Lucian

"YOU BROKE ME"—EMINEM (FEAT. BILLIE EILISH & NF)

"**Y**ou take care, kid," Griz said as he prepared to leave. He was getting released, and I experienced a sense of melancholy at the loss of the only friend I had there. Sure, he was a gruff bastard, not overly nice, but loyal to his word.

Over the past year, not a single motherfucker in the place fucked with me. Exactly as he promised. He'd also been a pretty cool cellmate, and I wasn't looking forward to who I got next. Not that I was scared; it was simply about trust. I'd gone from the clean-cut boy who had been terrified when the bars had first closed behind me, to a more hardened man. Not completely heartless, but Lila's death killed a little part of me that caused me to wall off my heart.

It also left me with a burning vengeance and a desire to see Luis Trujillo with a bullet between his eyes. The authorities had accessed the security feed in Lila's home and believed the cartel boss was with the men who had shot Lila and her family. Unfortunately, the footage wasn't extremely clear, and the bastard had rushed back to Mexico before he could be questioned or arrested and had successfully evaded extradition on several things since.

"I'll be fine. You stay out of trouble, old man," I said with a smirk.

"I think our last workout showed I'm no old man," he said with a slight lift at the corners of his lips. We'd worked in the shop together and had been workout partners every day after chow. I might've been a fit athlete when I came in, but I'd matured. Broader in the shoulders, I was stronger and buff as shit now. That might be another reason no one messed with me.

"Whatever makes you feel better," I said with a grin.

"You finish your degree. I'll be in touch when you get out. Contact the number I send. Tell them Griz told you to call. I think you'll be right at home there." He gripped my arm as the guards called for him. He had few belongings, since he'd left most of his shit behind for me.

I nodded but didn't make promises I wasn't sure I could keep. I'd been busting my ass to get my college degree since I'd gone to prison. He had pushed me when I wanted to give up. If I said it wasn't worth it because it wouldn't matter, he always replied with "bullshit."

"Keep your head down and you'll be okay," he said before following the guards out. I watched him leave with a heavy heart.

Over the year that Griz was there, we'd become as close as two convicts could be.

I also figured a few things out that I didn't tell him. Obviously, he knew there was something different about me. Still, there were certain things I didn't share with anyone.

One thing was that I could see dead people. No shit. Call them ghosts if you want, but a lot of them were more like residual energy. Occasionally, there was the type people imagined ghosts to be—one of those was both a pain in my ass and a reminder of my fuckup.

It also didn't take me long to figure out all I had to do was concentrate, will myself to disappear, and I did. Not that I let anyone know that—I wasn't an idiot. I also had no idea why I could do it.

Once he was gone, I did every program they offered, yet still, emptiness filled my days. Between school and the work I did, I didn't have a lot of time to think. Every penny I made that didn't go to my reparations to Kip's family, I saved.

It was after the sun went down that I dreaded. Each night, I was pulled into the distorted and dark world of my guilt.

It wasn't always the same. Some nights I was lying on the ground and someone started zipping me into a black bag. I kept trying to tell them to stop, that I was still alive, but the words wouldn't come out. Other nights I was in my truck and Kip was beating on the windows, begging me to save him. Covered in blood, with a twisted neck and mangled arm, he screamed as he slammed his fists on the glass. Red smears covered the barrier between us until I couldn't see him anymore.

Oh, and we couldn't leave out the nights when Lila haunted my dreams. Then I usually woke up, heart banging out an irregular beat, clawing at my neck to breathe.

"I don't know why you're still here," the hazy image said from the corner of the bench I was working at in the prison shop.

"Because my time isn't up," I quietly said so no one heard me but the fuzzy figure that wouldn't go away.

"That's not what I mean," it said.

In frustration, I paused and looked up at him after scanning the room to see if anyone was paying me any mind. "Well, what the hell else are you talking about?"

"You were supposed to be with me," he said, sounding confused.

My heart dropped. "What?"

"You weren't supposed to make it," he clarified in a matter-of-fact tone.

"Then why am I here?" I asked, but the figure appeared to shrug. I dropped my head back to the motor I was working on as my heart raced. "Okay, then why are you still here bugging me?" I muttered.

"Why can't you let it go? You didn't kill me. It was an accident, and it was my time to go."

"Yeah, well, the judge and jury saw things differently," I muttered.

"That's the other reason I'm here—it's my family's fault you're in prison. They shouldn't have pushed for it. I was already gone. You coming here didn't bring me back. Instead, they wasted your life to make themselves feel better about me being gone. I couldn't leave you here alone," he said, sounding sad.

Words escaped me, and he faded away to do whatever he did when he wasn't around.

I never knew when he'd be there. Rarely did I see him clearly, because it took a lot for him to be able to either talk or be seen. Both would take him out of commission for longer than he liked to leave me alone.

The days ran together, my only real friend a pain-in-the-ass spirit. Then one day about six months after Griz left, I found out I was actually being paroled. I'd earned an early release for my work in the prison and good behavior.

A little over two and a half years of my life, I spent in

a South Carolina prison. Far less than I thought I would, but enough that it changed the trajectory of my life forever. It made me wonder if things would've been different if I hadn't gone to that party. Or if I hadn't been so hardheaded and cut Lila loose. Would she still be alive? Would she have waited for me even though I told her not to, if she had been? The thing was, those were all things I'd never know.

"Are you leaving now?" I asked the figure sitting on my bunk as I packed.

"Maybe," he said.

I shook my head.

When I left the prison behind, I didn't look back. And my "friend" still dropped by from time to time.

"You gonna stick around here?" my ghostly friend asked as I took my break behind the shop.

"Haven't decided," I said as I lit up a cigarette—my one guilty pleasure.

"Those will kill you, you know," he said, causing me to choke on a laugh.

"I could be so lucky," I scoffed. He was pissed at that. Not that I could see his expression, but the crackle of energy around me said enough. Then the cigarette was extinguished.

"Asshole," I muttered. His laughter echoed, then faded away.

After almost five years from the day I'd been locked up, true freedom was within my grasp. My parole was coming to an end. Besides the obvious "no firearms," I also had no drinking, no drugs, no trouble. Most of it I could deal with, but damn, I wanted a fucking beer.

I'd spent my twenty-first birthday behind bars, and I

wouldn't be able to drink until my parole was completely up. It fucking blew, because many nights I could've used a stiff drink, but I wasn't risking fucking up and going back when I was this close. I knew they'd test me one more time before they cut me loose.

One more day.

I tossed the butt in the can by the back door and went back to work. Music filled the bays, and sweat ran down my back.

"Lucian! You have a phone call!" my boss, Miles, called from the door to the front waiting area and office. I didn't have a cell phone. Other than my parole officer, I had no one to talk to. I was lucky my landlady let me give my parole officer her number for my home number.

I wiped the grease from my hands and made my way up to the front desk.

"Yeah," I said when I put the receiver to my ear.

"Mr. Stone, I'm calling to confirm your appointment with Mr. Wallace tomorrow at 2:00 p.m." It almost made me laugh because it wasn't optional. At all. This was her polite way of saying "don't fuck up."

"Yeah, I'm tracking it. I'll be there."

"Very well. See you then." She hung up. My parole officer's secretary was abrupt, but hell, she dealt with ex-cons for three parole officers all day, every day. We weren't exactly being invited in for tea.

"Tomorrow's the day, right?" Miles asked when I replaced the receiver.

"Yep."

"I'm happy for you," he said as he scratched his gray beard.

"Thanks."

Miles and I weren't friends, because I didn't have any of those—unless you counted Kip's ghost. Yet, I believed he was being sincere. He'd hired me straight out of prison, and I hadn't missed a single day. I knew damn well I was a good employee and so did he. I never wanted to give him a reason to regret hiring me, but Kip's question burned at the back of my mind.

It sounded clichéd, but looking at the papers as I stood in the hot South Carolina sun, I experienced a true sense of freedom. I was done.

Holy shit.

Then I had a sinking sensation. Now what? I had no family—my mother had a heart attack the first year I was in and died. Not that she visited me once before that. My friends had slowly written me off, but that didn't bother me. We weren't the same people we were in high school. What the fuck would we talk about?

As I took a deep breath, I fought the feeling of drowning. Then I hopped the bus to go back to work.

The rest of my shift was hot, tiring, and long. My clothes were drenched in sweat by the time I clocked out. Another typical day.

"See you tomorrow," I said as I passed Miles on my way out.

"Have a good night," he said.

Since I didn't live far from the shop, I walked home. On the way, I paused at the door of a small bar that I passed hundreds of times before, never daring to stop in. With a small smile, I opened the door and stepped into the cool, dim interior.

I sat at the bar, and a disinterested bartender slapped a napkin in front of me. "What'll it be?"

For a second, I sat there blinking. What the fuck did I

want? I had no clue, so I said the first thing that popped in my head.

"Beer. Bud Light."

"Bottle or draft?"

"Bottle."

The guy nodded, popped the top off, and set it in front of me. "You starting a tab?"

"No," I said, unsure of the protocol. Fuck, I'd never been in a bar.

He told me the price, and I pulled out the cash. "Keep the change."

He left to help someone at the other end of the bar. For a moment, I sat there staring at the bottle, ignoring the hazy form to my left.

"It's not gonna drink itself," a gravelly voice said. I froze. Then I glanced at the guy who pulled up a stool next to me. He raised his hand to signal the bartender, ordered a draft, then glanced my way.

He was wearing a leather vest that had patches on it I couldn't read without staring.

"It's a good day for a beer," he said before he raised his glass to his lips. The foam stuck to his mustache, and he licked it off.

"Yeah," I replied awkwardly. It was as if the guy knew it was my first alcoholic beverage in five years. Damn, it was my first alcoholic beverage since becoming legal. I lifted the bottle to my lips, and the first taste hit my tongue. After that long, I expected it to be akin to Nirvana. Instead, it was just… beer.

"Good?" Kip asked as he sat next to me with his chin propped on the heel of his hand. I shot him a quick glare because I couldn't very well answer with people around or I'd look like a crazy person. Hell, maybe I was nuts.

The guy in the vest watched the TV over the bar as he drank.

When my bottle was empty, I set it on the now damp napkin and got off my stool. The guy looked in my direction, and I gave him a tight smile before I turned to leave. As I passed him, I saw the patch on the back. It said ROYAL BASTARDS with SAVANNAH, GA, on the bottom patch.

For a second, I almost paused to ask him if he knew Dennison. It had been a long time, though. In the time I'd been out, I'd never heard a word from the man who'd been my friend and said he was known in his club as Griz.

"Have a good ride," the guy said to me as I reached the door. I cast a glance over my shoulder.

"I'm walking," I said with a frown, wondering why I bothered replying.

He simply smirked at me and returned his attention to the TV as he took another drink.

When I stepped out into the sun, I had to blink a few times to adjust to the bright light. As always, I scanned the area. If prison had taught me anything, it was to pay attention to my surroundings.

That's when I saw a tatted-up guy standing next to two bikes. He was talking to a guy who leaned against a truck with an empty trailer. They both looked at me and gave me a chin lift in acknowledgement. One of them had a leather vest with patches on the back that read PROSPECT. The other guy had a T-shirt on that said Support Your RBMC with a pinup girl on a motorcycle.

Again, I was tempted to ask about Griz, but thought better of it as I gave them a chin lift of my own and continued the trek home.

I frowned when I turned the corner and saw a motorcycle

parked in front of the efficiency apartment I rented above an elderly lady's garage. I'd never seen her with a visitor that rode a bike.

"Weird," I muttered as I skirted around it, pausing long enough to appreciate the gleaming black paint. The bike looked older but well maintained.

I took the stairs two at a time and stopped short when I saw the plain white envelope sticking out of my screen door.

"What the fuck?"

I wasn't expecting the weight of the envelope. When I opened the door, it dropped to the ground with a clunk.

Glancing around suspiciously, I relaxed when there wasn't a soul in sight. Still, I kept an eye out as I unlocked my door and brought the envelope inside.

Staring at it like it might bite me, I debated opening it. With one fingertip, I flipped it over. Like the plain white paper might be different than it was two seconds ago.

Finally, I figured I had nothing to lose. I ripped it open and dumped the contents out. A small key bounced on the table before settling in front of me. Unfolding the papers, I found a single sheet of paper, a sticky note with a phone number, and a title document.

Kid,

Call Venom. Tell him Griz from Savannah gave you his info. He's the president, so be respectful. He's expecting your call. Learn to ride the fucking bike, then let it take you where you need to go. I hear Bumfuck, Iowa, is a decent place to be.

Take care of yourself.

Griz

P.S. Burn this when you're done—just in case. Haha.

Motherfucker. Griz had been true to his word. That explained the guys at the bar. *Holy shit.* I didn't question how he knew where I was staying, or the exact day I fulfilled my parole. Dude obviously had connections.

Holding the letter, I looked at the signed title. I didn't recognize the seller's name, and I wondered if it was a real person. It seemed legit, though.

A laugh escaped me. It grew until tears ran down my face as I held my stomach. Honestly, I had no idea why I was laughing but it felt good. Then I sobered and glanced at Kip's ghost.

"Do you ever see her?" I asked him, holding my breath as I waited for his reply.

He stared at me with a sorrowful gaze before he slowly shook his head. After I swallowed the lump in my throat, I nodded. It hurt that she wasn't able to come see me like Kip did. I would've settled for a message via Kip, because it would've been better than the nothing I had.

Making a decision, I did exactly as instructed. I called Venom and learned to ride. Then, the first chance I had, I hit the road for Iowa. Anything to get me away from the memories that plagued me in South Carolina. Crazy thing was, I couldn't seem to outrun them no matter how far I went and how much time had passed.

While my friend's ghost haunted me, I was also haunted by the memory of a blonde girl who was always the brightest star.

PART II

FIVE

Ghost

"ANYWHERE BUT HERE"—AARON LEWIS

As I pounded into Cookie, I gripped her hips hard. My fingers dug into her creamy flesh. Phoenix was groaning with his head thrown back as she sucked his cock like she had zero gag reflex.

When I was buried balls deep in hot, tight pussy, I could shed all the memories that plagued me every day. The ones that lingered in the periphery of my subconscious, waiting for me to slip up and think too much.

"Fuuuuck, Cookie. I'm gonna come. You swallow every fucking drop like a good girl," Phoenix said. She moaned around his cock, and that was all it took. As he was shooting his load down her throat, I gritted my teeth, rammed my cock deep, and filled the condom until I thought it might overflow.

With my fingers gripping the base of the rubber, I pulled out and smacked her pale ass. She giggled as she gave a last lick to Phoenix's dick like it was a freaking popsicle.

"Jesus fucking Christ, Cookie," he huffed, trying to catch his breath. "You're like a goddamn Hoover."

She chuckled as she licked her lips. The girl loved sex, and not a damn one of us were complaining. Well, not the single ones anyway.

"Flattery will get you everywhere, Phoenix," she said with a coy grin as she climbed off the bed. "Now, you two need to get the hell out. I need to get ready for my shift."

"Yes, boss," Phoenix teased as he tucked his shit away.

She turned back to us and smirked at Phoenix. "Mmm, you're gonna let me be the boss? Does that mean I can tie you up?"

Phoenix laughed. "Not a chance, sweetheart."

"Hmm, we shall see," she said with a wink before she closed the bathroom door.

"Holy shit," he said as he pulled his shirt back on and scratched his short beard.

"You can say that again," I said with a grin. "Let's go. We have a bike to deliver."

My life was perfect. I had free and willing pussy whenever I wanted it, brothers who would lay down their lives for me, and two wheels on the asphalt whenever I needed it. What more could I ask for?

Oh, yeah, maybe to quit thinking I saw Lila around every fucking corner. It had been twelve goddamn years. Like I said, those sonofabitchin' memories.

This was worse though. It was like her ghost was haunting me lately, and it was slowly driving me insane. Everywhere I went, I thought I saw her. Maybe it was time to take my annual trip to Savannah to visit Griz—and her grave on the way home. Except it was getting harder and harder. Time was supposed to lessen the pain, but in this case, it seemed to grow exponentially each year.

Yeah, there was that.

))

"Goddamn it, why is it so fucking cold?" I complained as Phoenix, Chains, Angel, and I went into the liquor store. It was only October, and it should be warmer than that shit.

"You're such a pussy," Angel teased, and I flipped him off. "Snuggle with Phoenix. He'll warm you up."

Phoenix was walking ahead of us and lifted both middle fingers.

We were having a party to celebrate Hawk's birthday. It was our job to pick up the alcohol. We had delivered a bike down in Des Moines, so we stopped there to pick shit up.

"What all is on the list? Are we gonna need another cart?" I asked as I grabbed one and started pushing it down the first aisle.

"Probably, but let's see how much we can fit in here first," Chains said as he started listing the shit we needed. Bottle after bottle went in the cart. A couple cases of beer went underneath. Phoenix, Angel, and Chains each had two cases apiece.

"Huh, guess one cart was good," I said with a grin.

We paid for everything and brought it out to Angel's truck. Once it was all loaded up, I paused. "I need to run into the grocery store next door."

"I gotta grab some shit too," Phoenix said.

"Hurry up," Angel said as he and Chains climbed in the truck.

We went through the automatic doors and split up.

I stood at the condom display, trying to decide on colors or ribbed. "Fuck it, I'll get both. It'll always be a surprise."

As I turned, I saw long pink hair accompanied by a perfectly rounded ass. She grabbed something off a shelf and dropped it in her cart. Then she tapped her pierced lip as she studied her options.

Her movements seemed so familiar, it gave me pause. It had been over ten years, but in my mind, I could see Lila's smile and the way she moved like it was yesterday.

Jesus, there I go again.

"Lila?" I whispered, but she didn't hear me. *Probably because it's never her, you dumbass.*

She turned in my direction, and my breath caught. The arch of her brows, the curve of her cheek, they had me getting a little lost in memories. As I always did, I had to tell myself to stop imagining.

Besides, the chick was tatted up. If Lila had been alive, I couldn't imagine her ever getting a tattoo—let alone sleeves of them. And pink hair? Never.

My heart hammered against my rib cage. Though I knew better, there was a part of me that always had to check. Like that little piece of me refused to admit she was gone—even years later. No matter how much time had passed, I saw her everywhere.

Stepping up the pace, I caught up with her in the next aisle. "Lila?"

If her step hadn't faltered for a second, I would've laughed at myself and paid for my shit. Swallowing the giant lump in my throat, I reached out and gripped her arm. My fingers tingled at the touch, and she sucked in a startled breath and spun to face me.

"Hey!" she said, frowning at the hand restraining her.

I released the breath I didn't realize I was holding. "I… uh, I'm sorry. You look so much like someone I used to know."

Her green eyes were wide, her face was drained of color, and she seemed shaken. Then again, a big dude she didn't know grabbed her in a grocery store.

The resemblance was uncanny, but where Lila's eyes had been crystal blue, this girl's were the color of a spring field. There was also a beauty mark by her mouth that Lila certainly never had. Her roots and brows were dark, and her hair transitioned to pink. Her nose was missing the bump Lila had from when she was babysitting and a kid head-butted her and was also pierced on both sides, along with her eyebrow and lip.

Though she wasn't Lila, she was still stunning. I wanted to kiss that beauty mark and look over her body for more. That sexy lip ring made me want to feel it under my tongue.

Despite coming to terms with my reality, I was compelled to stare. Fuck, she was hot. Not that I'd ever be one for a relationship, but I'd fuck all day, every day, if I could.

"It's okay. I get that a lot. Obviously, I'm this Lila's doppelgänger. Huh?" Her voice was husky and nothing like the lilting tone of the girl I'd loved. She gave a hesitant smile and pushed her hair behind her ear. When she did so, I noted there was no wedding ring.

"So we're having a birthday party for my brother tonight. You wouldn't be interested in going, would you?" After shoving away all the ridiculous comparisons, I shot her my best smile and tried to get my heart to slow down. She still looked enough like Lila that I wouldn't mind pretending for a night. Twisted, yeah. Probably even seriously fucked-up.

Sue me.

"Um, maybe. Where and when?" she questioned as her cheeks flushed dark pink and her gaze boldly raked over me.

"You have a pen?" I asked.

She dug in her massive purse and pulled out a cheap BIC pen. Waving it triumphantly in the air, she handed it over.

Giving her a smirk, I took her hand and wrote my phone number and the address of the clubhouse on her palm. Rippling feelings hit my stomach when our skin touched.

Damn.

As I finished, I glanced up and gave her a wink. She shook

her head with a repressed grin and dropped the pen back in her purse. Her hand seemed to shake, and she curled her fingers and fisted her hand as if she was holding the numbers.

I sucked in a deep and unsteady breath. "Fuck, I can't get over how much you look like her," I said before giving my head a quick shake.

She tugged on her lip piercing with her teeth. "It happens," she said with a coy smile.

"See you tonight," I said, hoping she didn't let me down. "Ask for Ghost when you get there."

Instead of replying, she gave me a tight smile that said "don't hold your breath."

Well, fuck. I thought I had her.

Phoenix and I paid for our shit and walked out into the brisk fall afternoon. We climbed in the truck, and Angel drove past the front of the grocery story to exit the parking lot.

As we passed the plate-glass windows, Angel stopped to let customers cross. Glancing in the store, I saw the chick at the checkouts. As the young clerk scanned her shit, she twisted her hair up and shoved that white pen through it. My lungs collapsed, and I nearly jumped out of the truck as Angel started moving.

"What the fuck are you doing?" Phoenix asked as he stared at my hand on the door handle.

In a bit of a daze, I glanced down to where my hand was ready to pull the lever. Then I shook off my crazy thoughts and laughed, playing it off. "Nothing. I'm good."

That night the chick never called or showed up.

Figured.

Oh, well. Probably for the best, because how fucked-up would it be if I started dating someone because they reminded me of my dead high school sweetheart.

SIX

Laila

"WHEN YOU WERE YOUNG"—THE KILLERS

"**W**ell, holy shit. I might've found something." My fingers flew over the keys as I pulled back layer after layer of information that didn't make sense. I downloaded most of it because I knew someone who might understand what I was looking at.

About a week ago, a guy who called himself Vladimir hired me to help find his sister. The authorities couldn't find anything that showed she was actually missing, since she'd gone on vacation and wasn't supposed to be back yet. They believed she simply didn't want her brother interrupting her trip, but he was convinced she was tied up in some bad shit.

It wasn't something I normally did, because I wasn't that good, but we'd met in a dark web chat room I'd been hanging out in for years. It had been a good source for small jobs. My heart had gone out to him. I didn't question how he'd gotten in, because that wasn't something you did in there.

I'd hit a lucky break the other day, but it had been a total fluke. When I was checking her credit card history, something seemed off. I started digging. Somehow, I tapped into a business that operated as a shell corporation for a few sketchy investments, some intellectual property, and several ships. There was money regularly transferred into the account from various other accounts and then disbursed into a single offshore account. Tonight I found out the shell corporation also owned several private islands in the Caribbean.

The reason I was looking at all was because she had said something to her brother about meeting a guy who was a lot older but had a lot of money. He had reportedly taken her on a luxury vacation. The clues Vladimir had were minimal and had led me on a wild goose chase at first. Then I figured out the older guy's name was a bogus identity that was listed in connection with the shell company. He actually worked as a car salesman.

After everything had downloaded, I made notes on what little I'd found that might help and sent it to him. I wasn't sure how much further I wanted to go with his missing sister, because it was getting way above my knowledge base. As far as the other files went, I planned to reach out to another contact to see what he made of them.

After I sent off the email to Vladimir, I poured my fourth glass of wine and started another search.

As I finished the last of the cheap wine, I scrolled through what had come up. Though it seemed crazy, the proof had been in front of me. Living and breathing proof. If I'd questioned it, his calling me Lila reinforced it.

"Of all the places I could've moved, I had to go to the same fucking area as Lucian Donovan Stone. Jesus help me." I shoved the computer away and buried my face in my trembling hands. Self-preservation screamed that I needed to pack my shit and move.

The problem was my traitorous heart—because the thought of intentionally leaving him again ripped me apart worse than the bullets that had pierced my chest eleven years ago. My fingertips slipped into the V-neck of my shirt and traced the scars hidden under tattoos. Every cell in my body screamed for him, and I didn't know what to do with that.

Simply seeing him set off a shifting in my chest. As if the broken pieces of my heart that I'd so haphazardly shoved back together were trying to click back into place properly.

I uncurled the fingers of my other hand and stared at the bold print on my palm. I'd been taken aback when he said it was his brother's birthday party that night, because Lucian hadn't had any siblings. It made me wonder if after he got out of prison, he found siblings he didn't know about.

Until I looked up the address. "Fuck, fuck, fuck," I muttered.

Lucian was a member of the Royal Bastards MC. I'd encountered them a couple of times since moving to Iowa, and they were intimidating to say the least. The Lucian I knew didn't know how to ride a motorcycle. Also, I didn't understand why he'd want to be a part of something that had a big stigma of being a gang. It seemed like it would be a bad idea, but I'd encountered a lot of shit over the years that told me to never question a thing. Yet to question everything.

Me: I need you to call me

Ryan: In the middle of something. You okay for about 30 minutes?

Me: Yes

55

It was insane that the only person I really considered a friend was a man I'd never actually met. Ryan was my case agent in WITSEC.

I'd been put in protective custody after the attack on my family. After all, I'd plainly seen the men who shot and killed my parents. Someone like Luis Trujillo wasn't a man who would let me walk away if he knew I was still alive.

My father had a lot of enemies, it seemed. To this day, I hadn't figured out what his connection was to Luis Trujillo. The only thing I knew was that they took all my father's files and his laptop. No one ever said why. The only thing I could figure was my dad had something on him.

It was easier to let the world think I was dead and put me in witness protection since Luis wasn't able to be tried, meaning I couldn't testify. The thing is, that wouldn't have mattered to Luis. He was the type of person that would've had me killed to tie up "loose ends." Meanwhile, I was initially babysat, then lived my life in hiding for over ten years while Luis greased palms in Mexico to avoid extradition.

It fucking sucked.

They sent me through school to be a nurse, but I ended up hating it. It was nothing like being a veterinarian, like I thought I wanted to do as a kid. Initially, I worked as a traveling nurse because it fed my lost and wandering soul. After too many bad patient experiences, I quit. I found I couldn't handle losing patients. I'd done a little waitressing, some bartending, and I'd worked several other jobs before I finally became a self-taught piercer. With that and the light hacking, I could travel to deal with the restlessness that came with not knowing who I was anymore. As long as I stayed dead, there was no reason for them to look for me. At least that's what we hoped. So far, it seemed to have worked.

The only other friend I would say I had was another person I'd never actually met. They went by the name Juggernaut. We never exchanged real names, but in one conversation he'd let it slip he was a guy. That's really all I knew about him, and he didn't know a lot about me. He knew me as Scarlett O'Hara.

I'd met him online in a shady-as-fuck chat room that I'd figured out how to enter my first year in hiding. No, I wasn't a hacker per se, but I had been bored. Entertaining myself, I found I had an aptitude for computers. Since the law couldn't seem to find my parents' killers, I thought I might be able to.

Then I'd done some sketchy shit to make money over the years. Little things like going in and changing grades. Or doing electronic surveillance for women who thought their husbands were cheating. Posting exposing shit on their social media accounts. The worst I'd done was emptying the bank accounts of a rich prick who had molested kids. I donated it all to every kids' program I could think of.

In a way, it was how I thumbed my nose at the law, since they couldn't find a way to bring Luis to justice.

I logged onto my computer running a Linux TAILS operating system and connected to the coffee shop next door's Wi-Fi network. Following all the steps I'd been taught, I opened up a virtual machine using virtualBox, then went through a VPN in combination with a proxy server. Once I was in the Tor browser, I sent the message through to Juggernaut. All the things I knew to protect myself—most of which I'd learned from him. I shouldn't have to worry, but I always did.

Me: I need some help

It would likely be some time before I heard back, so I'd reached for the screen to close my laptop when I heard a ping. Insanely, I was debating going to the party Lucian had invited me to attend. That sound quickly had me focused on my screen instead.

Juggernaut: With?

Me: Someone found out some of my history. How do I find out who it is?

Juggernaut: Seriously?

Me: Yes

Juggernaut: If they are good, you can't.

Me: Shit

Juggernaut: You're not a hacker like that, Scarlett. There's no way for me to explain how to even try. Do you want me to look into it?

I hesitated. There was no way I was giving him any more than he already had. Unless he already knew everything about me but was polite enough not to say so—or he could always be a psycho. Which was a little scary and made me question my sanity in talking to him at all.

Me: No.

Juggernaut: Let me know if you change your mind.

I wouldn't.

After closing out the connection with Juggernaut, I stared at Lucian's mug shot. I compared it to the changes I'd noticed in the grocery store. Young Lucian had been beautiful and bright—a brilliant football player with incredible potential. Thirty-one-year-old Lucian was devastatingly gorgeous. Shoulder-length dirty-blond hair, stunning blue eyes framed with lines that spoke of laughter and time in the sun. It had almost hurt to look at him.

And that body. Holy shit.

He'd grown a good two inches and filled out like a wet dream. All the years I'd forced myself not to look him up had nearly killed me. I'd told myself it wouldn't be fair, and it would devastate me to find out he was happily married with kids and a perfect life. I couldn't contact him because I didn't want to put him in danger, and I wasn't sure if he'd want to see me again anyway.

Before I could get up and drive to the address I'd already committed to memory, I filled my glass again. The bottle was empty, and I got up to grab the last one. After I'd run into Lucian, I'd grabbed three bottles because I knew I'd need them. I only stumbled a little bit on my way over to the fridge.

"How the hell would I explain why I hadn't contacted you all this time?" I asked the image of Lucian on my screen. He would hate me.

Sure, he asked me to go to the party, but did that prove he wasn't in a relationship? Maybe he was married. Those biker types weren't all loyal to their women. At least from what little I'd seen over the years. They all had those skanky women at their clubhouses. I'd done some bartending for a club in California once. Something-or-other Scorpions. Assholes.

It made me uneasy that Lucian was part of that life. It also turned my stomach a little. Not that I would ever be able to actually be with him again.

Suddenly, it was killing me to know if he was married. Chewing on my piercing, I searched public records. I blamed the wine for my weakness.

Nothing regarding a marriage.

Didn't mean he didn't have a live-in or a girlfriend. His address for his driver's license was the clubhouse. He had $257 in his checking account and $3,741 and some change in his savings account. If I knew if he'd gone to college, I could see what his grades were. That was as far as my "hacker" skills really went. I wished I'd picked Juggernaut's brain more.

I froze.

Did I dare?

I'd owe him, and that scared me a bit. My fingers fluttered nervously over the keys without typing anything. Finally, I grabbed myself by the lady-balls because I needed to know anything he could find for me. Something to hold close.

Me: Changed my mind. I need a favor

I waited.

Then waited some more. Dammit, he'd just been there. I sighed.

Juggernaut: I like the sound of this.

Me: Ugh.

Juggernaut: The suspense is killing me.

Me: I need you to look into someone for me.

Juggernaut: Gimme what you got.

Me: What's it gonna cost me, first?

Juggernaut: Don't know. I kinda like the thought of you owing me.

Jesus, that could be a really bad thing. Was it worth it? I filled my glass again.

Me: Yikes

Juggernaut: Don't worry, I won't rake you over the coals. Too much.

Me: Maybe this was a bad idea.

Juggernaut: Up to you.

Me: I'm not sending you nudes. I added an eye-rolling emoji as I giggled, despite the gravity of the situation.

Juggernaut: Bahahaha. That's what Pornhub is for.

Me: Ew

Juggernaut: Yes or No. I've got someone—I mean, something I'm in the middle of.

Me: Double Ew.

Juggernaut: tick tock.

Hesitant, I strummed my fingers on the tabletop. Then I took another sip of wine, then typed.

Me: Fine. Lucian Donovan Stone, age 31, last known residence, Ankeny, IA. Did prison time in South Carolina.

His chat had dots, then nothing, then dots, then nothing.

Me: Hello?

Juggernaut: Is this a joke?

Me: No… why?

Juggernaut: I'll get back to you.

His chat box went off-line.

"Well, that was weird." I finished the wine. When I sobered up, I'd likely regret what I'd done. At the moment, I was lost in memories of a young Lucian Stone.

My phone rang, and I quickly looked at the screen. I let out the breath I didn't realize I was holding.

"Yes," I said as I swiped the phone and held it to my ear.

"What's going on? Are you okay?" the voice said.

With a sigh, I explained what had happened.

"You can't stay there," Ryan said. Crazy how a disembodied voice was my best friend. I had no idea who "Ryan" was, because we'd never met in person. He became my case agent when my original one retired from the US Marshals three years ago. We only spoke over the phone and only on a burner phone.

"He believed I was Laila. But Ryan, I can't leave," I said, fighting the tears and the ache in my chest at the thought. The jolt I'd received the moment his hand touched mine had been heart-stopping.

He sighed heavily. "Fuck, Laila. This could be suicide."

"Everyone thinks I'm dead. Hell, after eleven years, Lila *is* dead. I highly doubt anyone is still looking for me, Ryan." I'd changed a lot about my appearance on top of changing my name and faking my death. I'd had the bump shaved off my nose and had a beauty mark tattooed on my face. I wore green contacts. I dyed my hair. I was covered in tattoos and piercings. I was so far removed from the teenage girl I'd been, it wasn't funny.

The one thing that had never changed was the fact that my heart belonged to Lucian Stone. No one had come close to him in all this time.

"About that...."

My stomach churned before it bottomed out. "What, Ryan?"

"There was some activity."

"What fucking activity? Don't beat around the goddamn bush. Spit it out!"

"Someone was searching for you, and we don't know who. They're good, and they accessed one of your files."

Blood rushed in my ears so loud that I didn't know if he was still talking. My heart hammered uncontrollably, and I couldn't breathe.

"What did they access?" I hated that my voice came out breathless and weak. That wasn't who I was anymore.

"Your medical records from after the shooting."

"But my medical records show I died."

"Your *real* records."

Fuck.

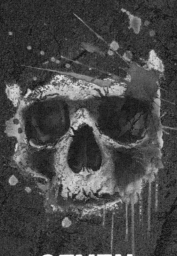

SEVEN

Ghost

"PARASITE EVE"—BRING ME THE HORIZON

With a groan, I rolled over in bed with my arm flinging to the other pillow as a pounding echoed in my head. My mouth tasted like something had shit in it. The room spun as I sat on the edge of the mattress. Incredibly, I was alone, and it caused me to frown.

Why the fuck was I alone? Oh, yeah, because I hadn't been able to get Miss Pink Hair out of my head. Lila's doppelgänger with the pink hair, tats, and piercings had filled my dreams. Drunken, X-rated dreams because I'd tried to drink enough to get her out of my head. Too bad it didn't work.

There was a knock on my door that had me holding my head and wincing.

"Fucking hell," I said as I stood and wobbled. The translucent figure sitting in my chair had its arms crossed. I flipped it off.

Then I shuffled to the door and opened it with a snarl. "Did you have to pound on the door so goddamn hard?"

Facet snickered. "I barely tapped on it. Put some pants on. That thing is staring at me," he said as he motioned to my dick.

"Hmph!" I grunted as I flipped him off and turned to grab my jeans from the floor. Muttering the whole way, I shuffled to the bathroom, pissed, washed my hands, then pulled them on. I zipped them and rummaged around for some Tylenol.

After dry-swallowing a couple, I came back out to see Facet sprawling in my chair, tapping his fingers nervously on the arm. I smirked at Kip sitting on Facet's knee, but in a flash, the figure was gone.

"What the fuck do you want?" I grabbed my phone to look at the time and groaned. "Jesus fuck, it's six in the fucking morning. Are you serious?"

"As a heart attack."

Falling back on my bed, I pulled my pillow over my face. "Come back in four more hours."

"Bro, I've waited as long as I could. Something weird happened last night."

"If you got me out of bed at six in the morning to tell me you lost your virginity last night, I'm gonna choke you."

"Ha. Ha," he sneered.

Unable to hold it in, I muffled my laughter in my pillow. "Find a new porn site?" I mumbled.

"You're a real dick, you know. Here I am trying to help you out, and you're being an asshole. Maybe I'll let this person find someone else to hack into your life."

That got my attention. The pillow went by the wayside, and I lifted my head to look at him with one eye closed, trying to focus. "The fuck you say?"

"Nothing. You know, I just look up porn," he airily announced as he stood. I threw the pillow at him, and it beaned him in the head.

"Fucker," he muttered.

"Talk."

"I've been talking to this person for years."

"What person? And this matters to me why? Move on to the part where someone wants to hack into my life."

He sighed, fell back into the chair, and ran a hand through his dark hair, causing it to stand up. "I don't think it's malicious, because I've never gotten that vibe from them."

"Okay? Tick-tock." I tapped my wrist as if I had a watch on.

He glared at me. "I taught the person damn near everything they know about the shady side of the internet."

"You mean the dark web?"

"Sort of. I don't think they are that deep in the dark part of it. Just kind of in the shade."

"If it's stealth shit like you do, don't candy coat it. It's dark shit to those of us that don't fuck with it."

Unfazed, he shrugged. "Last night she asked me to look into you."

He had my full attention.

"She? Did she say why?"

"I didn't ask. It was bad enough that I replied by asking her if it was a joke. It caught me so off guard, I messed up." He dropped his face into his palms as his elbows rested on his knees. That said something, because Facet didn't make mistakes.

"I don't understand."

"Me either. It really fucked with my head. She goes by the name Scarlett O'Hara, but that's not her real name, obviously. We were friends—or as much as two anonymous people can be on the web. I looked at her as a protégé, of sorts. Like I said, pretty much everything she knows is because of me. When we first met, she was fucking around in shit she had no business in, and I stopped her. We started talking. Honestly, I couldn't tell you why it started. Normally, I wouldn't bother to teach people what I know, because who wants to give away their knowledge? You know?"

"Then why did you? She could've been someone trying to get into your shit."

He scoffed. "I said I taught her everything *she* knew, not what *I* know. Trust me when I say I had the upper hand. She was truly harmless. A vagabond with no real home, originally born in California—or so I thought."

"Meaning?" I asked as unease grew and churned in my guts.

"Whoever created her backstory was good. There wasn't anything to raise eyebrows that it wasn't accurate. Everything checked out, and I didn't discuss my personal work with her. I truly saw no threat." He pinched the bridge of his nose.

"Until she asked about me."

"Yeah. I mean, I've been talking to her for almost ten years—since I was still in the military. I didn't even know you then. Plus, you've been here for much less than that. She obviously didn't befriend me to get info on you, so why now?"

"That's a good question. I'm assuming you know who and where she is?"

"Yeah. She moved to Des Moines about six months ago, but I didn't know. Never really had a reason to keep tabs on her every move. I would simply check on where she was occasionally. You know, make sure she was okay."

Alarm bells were ringing in my head, drowning out the pounding of earlier. It was as if I knew what he was going to say before the words left his mouth.

"Her name is Laila King, or it is now."

The roar of a freight train began to fill the room.

"When she asked about you, I thought maybe you had met

her at Royal Ink when you stopped by to see Chains. I mean she's a piercer, and I found out she put in an application there, but we didn't have an opening. It wasn't a far stretch. It was possible she had the hots for you." He shrugged. "But something didn't seem right. Call it a gut feeling, but things weren't making sense. After a lot of digging, and I mean a *lot*, in some very deep places I shouldn't have been, I found something interesting. Her name used to be Lila Kellerman before she went into witness protection."

I slid off the edge of the bed to the floor and gripped my hair as I curled into myself and the past swallowed me with a vengeance. I didn't hear Facet if he was talking to me, nor could I have said when he left the room.

The sound of the gavel banging drew my attention from my introspection.

"All in favor of taking on this job?"

Everyone pretty much voted yes. The ayes had it. Honestly, I didn't know what the exact job was, but I was fine with whatever the majority wanted. My mind couldn't process much more at that time. The Khatri Corporation was run by Rudra Khatri and his brothers. They owned several porn productions companies, and our chapter in New York City had actually done business with them at one time. What most people didn't know was that they also operated a high-class prostitution service too.

"Then Facet will start searching for the breach in the Khatri Corporation accounts, and we go from there." Venom's gavel hit the table again, and we were done. Several of the brothers hung around bullshitting. I had somewhere to be, so as soon as church wrapped up, I was on my feet.

"Ghost? A word," Venom said from the head of the table where he and Raptor still sat.

"Yeah?" I asked.

"Do you wanna tell me why Facet was looking into Laila King for you?" Venom asked as he crossed his inked arms and leaned back in his seat. He didn't look happy, but he wasn't poised to jump out of his seat at me, so that was good. I took a deep breath.

"She's a girl I met at the grocery store," I said, shrugging it off. I could tell by his expression that he knew there was more to it than that. He and Raptor stared, and I fought fidgeting like a grade-school kid in front of the principal.

"Okay," he finally said. "But run it past me first next time. Yeah?"

The lump in my throat made it hard to swallow around it, but I did and nodded.

"You can go," he said.

Happily.

I gave them a chin lift and left the room.

"Wait up!" Angel called as I walked down the hall to grab the keys to my car. I paused and glanced over my shoulder.

"Yeah?"

"Korrie is making dinner tomorrow night. She wants to know if you want to join us. I've invited Phoenix, Sabre, and the other brothers that aren't hooked up. Korrie thought you might enjoy a home-cooked meal at the house."

"Yeah, that sounds good. Thanks, bro."

"No problem." He looked like he wanted to say more but bit his tongue. Then he blurted out, "Are you okay? You've seemed off. I haven't heard you give anyone shit all day. It's weird, dude."

"I'm… I don't really know." I wasn't ready to discuss things with anyone. Facet knew by default, but not because I wanted anyone to know.

Lila was alive and had been hiding for over eleven years. It didn't make sense. At least not until I remembered the details of the murder

I went in my room, snagged my keys, then knocked on Facet's door.

"Come in!" he called out.

When I stuck my head in, he was at his desk, staring at his multiscreen computer.

"Hey. Do you think I could get Laila's address? If you can find it for me?"

He choked on his energy drink. "*Can I?*"

I almost laughed at his affronted expression. "Okay, sorry... I mean, would you? I know you have a lot going on with this new job we got."

"Yeah. I will. But do you wanna tell me why? It's been eleven years—you don't know her anymore."

Not meeting his gaze, I scratched my chin. "She used to be my girl."

"That's kinda what I figured after reading Lila Kellerman's story, but that doesn't tell me why you want to see her now?"

I scuffed my shoe against the concrete floor, then looked up at him. "It was before I went to prison. I ditched her when I found out how long I was going away for. Didn't want her wasting five years of her life waiting on me. Then I read she was murdered with her parents when I was in. I'd never felt so helpless. You can't exactly grieve in prison. Then I ended up getting out early, and I regretted ending things with her. I kept asking myself if things could've played out differently if I wouldn't have broke things off."

"Damn. But bro, you have to know that it wouldn't have changed anything. You couldn't control what happened back home, when you were in prison."

"It was when I was in prison that I found out I could become a ghost. I thought she was dead."

"Double damn."

"So, um, could I have her address?"

"Do you think that's a good idea? Until I know more about her situation, it might not be a good idea for her to be seen with you. She's in WITSEC for a reason. What if the US Marshals or the feds are watching her or some shit?"

"I'm not going to talk to her. I just need to…." What did I need? I had no fucking idea. My head was reeling. My thoughts were an emotional jumble that I couldn't seem to organize.

He sighed but clicked a few keys, then scratched out something on a Post-it Note. He handed it to me with a frown. "Be careful. I already got my ass chewed for looking into her for you. Venom would have my ass if he knew I hacked into secure government servers. I'd get center punched if he thought I sent you into danger."

"How much danger could one woman be?"

He arched a brow.

I had no idea how much I'd rue those words.

EIGHT

Laila

"WE WILL NOT GO QUIETLY"—SIXX:A.M.

As I stepped outside and ensured the door was closed, a dark shape caught my eye. I frowned as I looked across the street at the Challenger I'd seen parked there a few nights this past week. I'd never seen it before the first night, but it was always empty and not always in the same exact spot. So either I had a new neighbor, someone got a new car, or maybe someone had a new significant other. I memorized the license plate to look up when I got back to the house.

Being cautious of my surroundings had become second nature over the years. I tossed my purse in the passenger seat and climbed in, started my car, and drove to the tattoo studio in historic downtown Des Moines.

It didn't appear anyone had followed me, so I breathed a sigh of relief. I wanted to laugh at my overactive imagination. The electronic doorbell went off when I went inside.

"Be with you in a minute!" a voice yelled out from the back.

"It's just me!" I replied as I went around the wall to the small space they had set up for me. It was a temporary gig, so I wasn't worried about having a big space. I unlocked the toolbox I used and pulled out what I needed for my appointment.

"You're early," the sexy voice said. I glanced up and smirked. Leo was hot as hell but very much in love with his wife.

"Yeah, I figured I better be here in case they showed up early."

He gave me a chin lift. "I made coffee, and Devlin brought in some stupid-ass little Bundt cakes if you want one."

"You got chocolate?"

"Does a bear shit in the woods?" Devlin asked as he stepped up behind Leo, shoving a delectable-looking little cake in his mouth with a smile.

I snorted out a laugh. Leo left to return to his room.

"You got plans after we close?" Devlin asked as he lifted his coffee cup to his lips.

"No, why?"

"Thought you might like to stop off at Bruno's afterward to have a drink."

He'd been hinting at us getting together for months. Sure, I flirted, but I hadn't planned to really pursue anything. Work hookups often got messy. Yet he was handsome, and I'd be a liar if I said I hadn't considered sleeping with him. At least up until a few days ago.

Things had changed.

Lucian was here.

Ugh! It didn't matter! Nothing could happen with Lucian regardless of my feelings. He couldn't know I was here. Instead, I told myself I only wanted to find out if he was happy and then I'd probably pack my shit and leave again.

Except every time I thought that, it was as if someone had shot me all over again. It was crazy. Especially considering there wasn't anything I could do about it. At least not until I figured out who was looking into me. I made a mental note to contact Ryan to see if there were any new developments regarding the access to my records.

"You know? Yeah. I think that's just what I need." One drink wouldn't hurt. It also might get my mind off Lucian.

The bell chimed, and I glanced at the clock. "That's probably for me," I said as I brushed past him. The scent of his cologne was light but teased my senses. It was nothing like the intoxicating one that had poured off Lucian in the grocery store. That had been a blend of some woodsy cologne, oil, gas, and the faint scent of cigarette smoke. An odd combination, but one that had me wanting to press my nose to his neck and inhale deeply.

"Cool," he said from behind me as I greeted my customer.

"Hey, Felicity. Are you ready for this?" I asked the young, nervous-looking woman.

She glanced at her boyfriend, then back at me.

"Sure," she said with a shaky smile.

I motioned for them to follow me back.

"Sorry, it's pretty small in here, but your boyfriend can sit in the chair there," I said as I motioned to the seat positioned in the corner of my space.

"Hell, yeah," he said as he settled into the chair.

I finished setting my supplies on the small stainless steel rolling table as I explained the process to her.

"The barbells I'm going to put in are longer than what you'll wear after you heal. This will allow for swelling in the nipples. It will go down, but initially you'll need the extra room on the bar."

Wide-eyed, she nodded.

"Okay!" I said with a bright grin. "Remove your shirt and bra. I need to mark you to ensure we're straight."

She did as I said and nervously balled her shirt up around her bra.

"Go ahead and sit on the table," I instructed as I motioned to the massage table.

She stood and held the wadded-up shirt protectively against her stomach. Then, I grabbed a small level. People laughed at me that I took piercing to such precision, but I hadn't gotten to where I was without being meticulous.

I held the level to her nipples and made a mark on either side of each one with a surgical marker.

"How does that look?" I asked her as I passed her a hand mirror. She studied the marks and finally handed it back to me with a nod.

"Are you sure you want to do this?" I quietly asked her one last time. It seemed like her boyfriend was more excited about the process than she was.

She glanced down at her breasts, then at her boyfriend. "Is it gonna hurt?"

I wanted to pinch the bridge of my nose and groan. What I wanted to say was "No, not at all. I'm only shoving a sharp needle through each nipple, followed through by a bar that I will need to screw on and tighten. Nothing to worry about."

Instead I gave her a reassuring smile. "It's not gonna feel great, but it will be over quick. That I can promise."

I was true to my word. The procedure was over with minimal mess, and Felicity handled it like a trooper. After going over the care instructions with her, I finalized her payment and showed her and her boyfriend out.

It didn't stop there. By the time we closed, I ended up with three walk-ins and two other scheduled appointments. Leo locked the door, and we walked to our cars.

"See you guys tomorrow," Leo said as he climbed in his sleek car. We all waved.

"Meet you there?" I asked Devlin.

Devlin stopped by my car and rested an arm over the roof. His dark hair fell over his forehead, and he grinned. The cutest damn dimples popped with that smile. In another world, I could've completely fallen for him.

"You could always ride with me and maybe, oh, I don't know… stay at my place tonight." He leaned in and ducked his head to look me in the eye.

A car door slammed loudly, and we both looked around.

When I saw the same Challenger that'd been at my place parked about four cars down from us, I sucked in a sharp breath. My heart started to pound, and I nervously scanned the area, but there was no one in sight except a couple walking down the sidewalk toward us from the opposite direction. No way was it a coincidence though.

"You ready?" Devlin asked, dismissing the sound.

"Yeah, I'll follow you," I said, giving him a smile that I sure as hell didn't feel. Chills chased over my skin from head to toe.

It took us a few minutes before we were pulling into Bruno's gravel lot. It was close enough that we could've walked, but we would've had to go back in the opposite direction of where we both lived.

As we walked toward the small bar, Devlin rested his hand on my lower back. I swear to God, I heard a growl and felt what seemed like hot air across my neck. It sent a shiver down my spine, and I darted a glance around again. We were alone in the lot, and there were about ten other cars there but no people.

A familiar scent blew on the light breeze, and I hurried inside.

Shaken, I settled on a stool at the bar. Devlin and I placed our orders, and he started talking, but I barely caught what he was saying. The feeling of being watched weighed heavy on my shoulders, and I wanted to go home.

"Thanks for buying my drink," I said as I finished and set the glass of ice down on the napkin.

"You're leaving, aren't you?" Devlin said with a crestfallen expression. I gave him an apologetic smile and nodded.

"I'm sorry, I'm beat. I really want to go home and soak in a hot bath. I slept like crap last night." To soften the blow, I pressed a friendly kiss to his cheek, and my glass flew across the bar and shattered on the floor.

"Oh my God! I'm so sorry, I must've bumped it," I said to the disgruntled bartender. Though I didn't remember making contact with it after I set it down, I must have, and I felt like an ass.

"It's all good," he said, though it didn't seem like he meant it.

"I'll walk you out, at least," Devlin offered as he stood from his stool.

"Sure," I replied, and we went out into the night.

When we reached my car, I opened the door, and Devlin waited until I was safely in and pulling out of the lot. A quick glance in my rearview showed him standing with his hands in his pockets watching me drive away. Then when I looked forward, I passed the Challenger parked on a side street.

"Oh fuck. Fuck, fuck, fuck!"

Already running through my escape plan, I drove straight home. Paranoia made me think every car was following me. Regardless if it was true or not, my gut was telling me something was very wrong.

I got lucky and found a spot on the street in front of the small record shop where I had an efficiency apartment upstairs. All the shops had been remodeled, and the upper levels had been converted to small but sleek apartments.

I took the stairs two at a time.

After locking my door, I opened the closet and pulled out my suitcase. Ripping things off the hangers, I shoved them inside. The bedside table that doubled as an end table when my futon was in couch mode was quickly emptied next.

The few toiletries I had in the bathroom went into a plastic grocery sack and got added to the growing contents. My purse was last. Once I was satisfied I had what I needed, I zipped it shut.

My laptop went into my backpack along with my identification papers and the rest of my equipment before I set it on the futon. The kitchen items I had were cheap and expendable, so I didn't worry about them.

There was a knock on my door, and my heart jumped into my throat as I froze.

"Laila?" a voice called, and relief made my shoulders sag. "Are you home?"

Looking through the peephole, I verified it was my landlady, Mrs. Aberdeen, from across the hall.

"Hey," I said, giving her a bright smile but keeping the door closed enough she wouldn't see my suitcase sitting in the middle of the floor.

"Laila, dear, could I trouble you for one of your little coffee cup things?"

I gave a nervous laugh. "It's eleven at night. Are you sure you want the caffeine at this time?"

She smiled. "My brother just flew in unexpectedly, and he's dying for a cup, but I'm out. I planned to go to the store tomorrow morning."

"Sure. Just a second," I said as I closed the door most of the way. I quickly grabbed the box of pods, since I wouldn't be taking them, and brought it to her.

"Oh! I only needed one," she said as she tried to take one and give me the box back.

"No, you keep them. I'm trying to cut back on my caffeine. I bought some decaf ones, and those were going to go to waste."

She gave me a hug. "Thank you so much, and good for you. I wish I had that much willpower."

With a wave, she crossed the hall and went inside. She had the only full-size place of the four apartments in our building. She and her husband had owned the record store downstairs. When he died unexpectedly, their son took over, but she still lived in their two-bedroom apartment.

Once I secured the door, I scratched out a note for her and left it on the counter. I'd miss her, and I felt bad for running out without notice, but she could keep my deposit.

As I glanced at my suitcase and backpack, I had the sad thought that at twenty-nine years old, it was pitiful that my entire life fit in those two bags.

I'd contact Ryan once I was on the road. He messaged earlier to tell me they wanted to assign me a new identity again because of the breach. I told him to do what he had to because I was simply tired. He'd be relieved I was leaving, but I wouldn't tell him I didn't plan to go much further than Waterloo. Though I knew it was stupid, the thought of being too far from Lucian made my heart hurt.

Once again, I was starting over.

NINE

Ghost

"WHAT IT TAKES"—ADELITAS WAY

Unrealistic fury burned in my veins when the asshole touched her as they went inside. I was right on her heels, but she had no idea. Just as she had no idea I'd been watching her from my car for the last week. One of the perks of being able to disappear, I supposed.

When she stood to leave and pressed a kiss to his cheek, I couldn't stand it, and I swept her glass to the floor.

Devlin watched her drive off like a lovesick puppy, and I hated him a little as I wondered if he'd fucked her. It made me feel like an asshole, because he was a ladies' man but a nice guy. Before Chains had come back from the army and started doing our ink, Devlin had actually done one of my pieces.

Not caring about him anymore, I walked down the street and slid behind the wheel of my car. Once I made it to her street,

I parked again. Antsy, I tapped the wheel. As I did every night, I debated going up to her apartment and confronting her. A couple of times, I'd actually stood outside her door like a crazy stalker. My hand swiped roughly over my mouth as I fought her draw.

I had no idea how to feel. Because no matter how bad I wanted to see her again, I was afraid of scaring her away. My life had become that of a psycho stalker as I watched her from afar—torn between longing and rage.

My phone rang, and I glanced down to see it was Facet. "Yeah," I abruptly answered.

"Where are you?" he demanded without his usual joking.

"Busy. What do you need?"

"This is bad. So fucking bad. I can't believe I didn't catch this sooner. If you still care about her, you need to pick up Laila. Like, now."

"Why?" I asked, but I was already getting out of my car and crossing the road to the record shop. The back door leading upstairs was insanely easy to pick.

"She's the breach in the Khatri accounts. Turns out, we weren't the only ones they hired—the other people are some really sick fucks. I tried to send her a message but she's off-line. Thing is, they found her, so unless you want her to end up dead for real this time, you better move quick."

"Shit!" I said as I took the stairs two at a time, praying with each step. The gig was up, and I had to hope she'd go with me without a fight.

"I don't know how much time you have," he said as I heard him clicking away at his keys.

When I stopped outside the door I'd already stared at several times like a lunatic, I raised my hand. "I'll call you back," I softly said as I ended the call and shoved it in my pocket.

Angry, I cursed when she immediately opened the door. It was a sloppy move, and she was lucky it was me.

"Did you need the creamer too?" she asked with a smile that fell when she realized I wasn't who she was expecting. Immediately, she tried to slam the door, but my hand shot out to stop her and I pushed my way in.

She backed away, holding her arms out as if that could fend me off. My eyes swept the tiny but immaculate apartment.

"Going somewhere?" I asked with a cocked brow when I saw her packed suitcase and backpack.

"What are you doing here? How did you get in?" she asked, acting like she had no idea who I really was. "I'll call the cops," she added, holding up her phone and pointing a shaking finger at the screen. Too bad she was a shitty actress.

"You actually made my job easier," I said as I grabbed her backpack and slung it over my shoulder. "Jesus, what the hell do you have in here?" I muttered as I hooked it over both shoulders. The plain black pack was heavy as fuck. Then I picked up the suitcase.

"What are you doing?" she demanded in a panic as she rushed to take the bags. My hands gripped them tighter, and I had to fight the noticeable jolt I experienced when her hand touched mine.

"Let's go," I ground out as I wrapped my free hand around her arm.

"Stop!" she whisper yelled as her wild eyes darted toward the door across the hall. "I can't go with you!"

"Lila, the Khatri's found out you got into their accounts. Now, you have two fucking seconds to get your ass in gear, or I'm tossing you over my shoulder and carrying you."

Her jaw dropped in shock, but I wasn't waiting for her to process. I crouched to toss her over my shoulder like I promised.

"What? No!" She swatted at me.

"Then let's go. Unless you want me to leave you to whoever it is that found you," I said through gritted teeth.

That got her attention in a hurry. Her face may have blanched, but she hurried to shut the door and damn near ran down the stairs ahead of me.

"Wait!" I snapped before she burst out the door at the base of the stairs. Panic vibrated off her in waves as wide eyes stared up at me.

"Let me make sure the coast is clear," I whispered.

Cautiously, I cracked the door and glanced down the alley that ran between the record shop and a coffee shop. When all seemed quiet, I gripped her small hand in mine and headed to my car at a furious pace.

Halfway across the street, I saw the translucent figure waving at me to hurry. "Now you show up to help," I muttered to the vague figure that had appeared.

"Who are you talking to?" she asked me as her gaze darted around.

I didn't bother answering, because she wouldn't understand. I yanked open the passenger door. "Get in."

I thought I heard her mutter, but she did as I said. I was popping the trunk as I shut her door. The suitcase was quickly tossed in, and I reached up to close it when I had the wind knocked out of me. In shock, I glanced down and saw dark crimson spreading across my shirt.

"Fuck!" Teeth gritted, I rushed to the driver side. Another burn hit my arm as I dove in. In no time at all, I had the car started, rammed it in gear, and was tearing out as the back window shattered and she screamed.

"Oh my God! Oh my God! Someone's shooting at us!" She spun in her seat to see. Headlights appeared behind us, and I downshifted to turn the corner. They followed me and started to close in. Another shot was fired.

"Get your fucking head down!"

"You're bleeding!" she exclaimed as she ignored my instructions. "Oh fucking Jesus!"

Unbuckling, she whipped off her T-shirt.

"What the fuck are you doing?" I shouted as I raced through the darkened streets trying to lose the car behind us.

"Putting pressure on your wound before you bleed out!" She shoved the wadded-up fabric against the wound on my upper chest. It hurt like a motherfucker.

Using the voice command, I called my president.

"This better be good," he said. "Because your ass is in a sling. I got a call from Facet."

"I need backup! I've been shot. Car on my ass, still shooting!" I gasped as I fought passing out. I rattled off where we were and the direction we were heading.

In the background, I heard rustling and the sound of boots hitting the ground. "Call Raptor," I heard him say and Loralei's muted reply.

He relayed everything to her and then was back with me. "Stay with me. Keep telling me where you are. We're on the way."

I nodded, though I knew he couldn't see me.

Next I heard his truck start up and the screeching of tires.

Another quick left followed by a right, and I was racing down the highway. The car was still on my ass. The first exit I came upon, I pulled off, whipped a bitch, and got back on the highway the other direction. Each time, I told Venom where I was. Thankful for my Hellcat, I shifted gears, hit the gas, and we pulled away from the car behind us.

Black dots broke through my vision, and a cold sweat trickled down the back of my neck.

"I think I see you coming. If that's you, flash your brights," I heard Venom say, and I did as instructed. There were two other vehicles behind him, and they split after they passed, taking up both lanes.

"They're gonna hit them head-on!" Lila shouted.

"No, we're not, darlin'," Venom said over the speakers.

In the rearview, I glanced up in time to see the car swerve and run off into the ditch, where it rolled. That was all I saw because I wasn't stopping.

"Get to the clubhouse! Angel's waiting," Venom instructed.

"Roger that," I said as I winced.

It seemed to take forever, but I knew it was likely only minutes before we were sliding sideways through the gate and stopping in front of the clubhouse doors. She was out of her side in a flash, and I almost fell to the ground when she ripped open my door.

"Lucian! Oh fuck! Lucian!" she yelled at me as she tried to get me out of the car.

"We've got him, babe," I heard a calm voice say before I was lifted and my arms were slung over Angel's and Phoenix's shoulders. The movement sent blinding pain through me, and I gasped.

Feet nearly dragging, they quickly brought me to the infirmary. As I was laid on the gurney, I coughed, and blood sprayed across my stomach and onto my thighs.

"If you make it, you are in such deep shit. Venom is *pissed*," I heard Phoenix mutter as he helped Angel.

"If? I'm offended," I heard Angel throw back at him.

"Why would he be pissed? We'd all do the same for our ol' ladies," Voodoo questioned from next to Laila.

She gasped, and I saw Venom pass her to enter the room.

"That true?" Venom asked me.

"Fuck, I hope so," I groaned as white-hot pain burned in my lungs and I coughed again.

"Oh, it's true," Voodoo insisted, but his voice sounded like it had been electronically slowed down.

The room was spinning as the cold blades trailed over my skin where they cut my shirt off. My head lolled to the side to see Lila with tears streaming down her face and hands over her mouth. I realized she was standing there in front of my brothers in her bra, and possessive rage bubbled within me.

"Get her out of here and give her a shirt," I mumbled before I passed the fuck out.

When I came to, my head was pounding, and my mouth was dry as the Sahara. I groaned as I tried to sit up.

"Don't get up! What do you need?" I heard her whisper as her small hand splayed over my bare chest.

Blinking to clear my vision, I croaked, "Need water."

A bottle was thrust into my hand, and I fumbled to open it. After one of Angel's healings, I was always dizzy and disoriented. Despite her order, I sat on the edge of the bed, bare feet hitting the cool floor and causing me to hiss. I fucking hated cold.

"Oh, shit. Here, let me do that," she said and took the bottle back. I heard the crack of the lid turning as it broke the seal. "Careful," she said as she gently held it to my lips.

Like I hadn't drunk in days, I swallowed every drop. My hair fell over my face as I dropped my head.

When I raised it, she was sitting in front of me, lips pulled between her teeth and green eyes wide and worried. My gaze traced her slight figure practically drowning in one of my Pink Floyd T-shirts as she sat on my desk chair next to the bed.

"I have no idea what happened tonight. I'm pretty sure I'm stuck in a crazy nightmare or I've lost my fucking mind," she finally whispered. I snorted at her cussing, because it was so out of character for the Lila I remembered.

"Oh, I can assure you, you're very much awake." Despite my assurance, she sat there blinking owlishly at me.

"I have questions," she finally said.

"Yeah? Well, so do I. You go first."

"How did you know to come and get me tonight?" she started with.

"Facet was tracking a hacker that got into a client's bank account and computer files. His search led him to you. He found something that told him they found you and were going after you tonight."

"Facet is who was after me?" she asked.

"No." I didn't give her anymore.

"H-H-How did that guy do that?" She waved a slender hand in the air as she motioned to my chest and arm. As an afterthought, I glanced down to see he'd done a pretty damn good job of patching me back together. There was barely a mark on my skin.

"Long story. Let's just say that a lot of my brothers have certain... abilities. We'll talk more about that later, but you can't tell anyone about what you saw."

"I wouldn't!" she indignantly replied. Searching her eyes, I was finally satisfied she was telling the truth. I took a deep breath, slowly exhaling before I nodded.

"My turn." My gaze locked on hers before I demanded, "Where the fuck have you been? And why didn't you reach out to me once in the past eleven years?"

She gasped. "What?"

"No. Goddamn it, Lila, I fucking *mourned* you!" I lashed out.

She clenched her teeth as a spark flickered in her eyes and her nostrils flared angrily. "You don't get to do that, Lucian. You're the one who fucking threw us away—threw *me* away. You think I didn't mourn you every time one of my letters was returned to me unopened? Each one was a knife to the goddamn heart! I loved you with every fiber in my being!"

It shouldn't, but her use of the past tense was like getting shot all over again.

"They said you were shot! They said you fucking *died*, Lila!"

She whipped off the shirt as she shot to her feet. "I was!" she shouted as she slapped her hand to her chest where the tattoo of a phoenix was emblazoned on her skin. "And Lila *did* die eleven years ago. Along with every scrap of innocence and youth she possessed. I go by Laila, but honestly, half the time I have no fucking clue who I am!"

Her chest was heaving, and angry tears glistened on her lashes as I stood. I towered over her, and she boldly stared at me, not backing down.

Brows furrowed, I reached out and ran my fingertips lightly along the lines of the phoenix. At the first touch, she sucked in a sharp breath. My hand paused, and I searched her eyes for permission.

Her breasts rose and fell in the black lace bra as I resumed when she didn't stop me. The puckered flesh was barely noticeable if you didn't know it was there. The color in the design was slightly off and blurred a bit in places, but it was a beautiful cover-up over the scars she indeed carried. The creature's head sat nestled at her cleavage, and the wings spread over the curves of her breasts and feathered under her collarbones.

Next, I skimmed along her collarbone and up her neck. In near wonder, I trailed my fingertips over the beauty mark with question.

"Tattooed," she whispered.

My fingers traced the slope of her nose.

"Rhinoplasty."

My hands cradled her face to lift her gaze to mine as I

stared into green eyes that looked nothing like the crystal blue I remembered.

"Colored contacts. And before you move on to my hair and brows, it's dye." She stepped out of my reach and pulled the shirt back over her head. Staring at the ground, she wrapped her arms around herself protectively.

"Lila," I began.

"No. Laila," she corrected.

"Because of the song?" I asked, already knowing the answer. She silently nodded, and that hit me like a boot to the guts too.

There was a knock at the door. "Come in," I called out as I pull back my hair and wrap a band around it.

"You doing okay?" Angel asked. His gaze flickered from me to Li—Laila.

"Yeah," I murmured as I nodded.

"Good. The officers just had a meeting. Venom wants to see you."

Opening a drawer, I pulled out a shirt from the top and put it on. Then I grabbed socks and sat down to tug them on along with my boots. "I'll be back," I said to Laila, but Angel interrupted.

"Pres said she better have her fucking ass sitting there with you," he said cautiously.

Well, hell.

TEN

Laila

"TRAIN"—3 DOORS DOWN

"You two have some explaining to do," Venom demanded. "I'm not explaining shit. You don't know a damn thing about me," I snarked.

Ghost face-palmed next to me, and I heard him whisper, "Aw fuck."

Voodoo snickered, and I'm pretty sure Venom had steam coming out of his ears, but I didn't care.

"Considering you dragged my fucking club into your issues, and one of my brothers into your shit, I'd say it's damn well my business. Otherwise, pack your shit," the man who had introduced himself as Venom instructed in a deceptively calm tone.

"I told you, it's his ol' lady," the guy named Voodoo mumbled, and Venom shot him a glare. Voodoo simply shrugged. I had no idea what that meant exactly, but I assumed it meant I was Lucian's—Ghost's—old girlfriend.

"Fine. I was looking for a client's sister who went missing while she was in the Bahamas. She told her brother that her new boyfriend was taking her on a romantic trip. Two days in, she didn't call and wouldn't answer her phone. Her brother called the boyfriend, and he kept saying she was busy—massages, napping, excuse after excuse before he quit answering too. It was really a fluke that her receipts and credit card led me from one minuscule trail to another until it connected to the bank accounts of some bogus shell corporation. Accessing the accounts allowed me to backdoor into a computer system. There was a bunch of shit that didn't make sense to me, so I copied the files to go through them. I gave him what I'd found except for the files, because I didn't know if they would help at all. There was the possibility there was no connection, so I didn't want to get the guy's hopes up—especially if he didn't know what he was looking at either," I said with a sigh as I rested my forehead on the heel of my hand.

The men sitting around the table were scary as hell. A few I recognized as the ones I crossed paths with briefly in Des Moines. A totally tatted-up one I remembered being the one I talked to at a shop when I first got to town. If I remembered correctly, he went by Chains. Holy shit, if I'd taken a position there, I might've run into Lucian earlier. My head was spinning.

"Here's the thing, Scarlett, um, I mean Laila," the guy who introduced himself as Facet said. I frowned as I tipped my head and studied him. "They know you got in. They discovered the breach but couldn't figure out how it happened or who you were. The Khatri organization hired us to find you, but it turns out they hired someone else too."

"How did you know I was Scarlett?" I asked him with

narrowed eyes, momentarily disregarding the fact that he said someone else was looking for me.

He had the nerve to look sheepish. His dark hair was shaggy and obscured his eyes, so it was difficult to determine the color. "Uh, well, because I'm Juggernaut."

My shoulders sagged as I closed my eyes, remembering I'd asked him to look into Lucian. "Of course you are."

"Crazy enough, you inadvertently led us to someone we've been trying to find. The thought that we were so close to them and had no clue makes me nauseous," Facet said. Knowing how good he was at what he did, I could imagine how frustrated he must be that he couldn't find something that I did. Though I had no idea what it was.

"So now what?" I asked as I searched the faces of the men at the table.

"Now we have some things to discuss and plans to make," the man called Venom said as he smoothed his short-cropped salt-and-pepper beard. He'd introduced himself as the president.

"What about me? Can I leave?" I asked. Lucian tensed where he'd been silently brooding next to me.

"You want to leave? Just like that?" Outrage colored his tone, and I inwardly cringed. Hell, no, I didn't want to leave him, but how could I stay?

"I'm sorry, but it wouldn't be safe for you to go," Venom said apologetically.

"But this is what I do. I'm a pro at disappearing," I rationalized. It wasn't something I enjoyed, but it was my way of life.

I was torn between wanting to be close to Lucian and wanting to beat him over the head with something. I'd spent the last ten years intentionally avoiding looking him up, but now that I was in his orbit again, it was difficult to break free of his gravitational pull.

It was as if the past eleven years apart didn't exist.

"This is un-fucking-believable," Lucian said as he stood, shoving his chair back in the process.

"Ghost! Sit down!" Raptor demanded, but Lucian was already slamming through the heavy wooden doors. Raptor stood to go after him, but Venom shook his head and grabbed his arm.

"Let him go."

"I need to notify my case agent to let him know I'm okay," I said as I fought the need to go after Lucian. They had taken my phone the second they ushered me out of the room they brought Lucian to after he'd been shot.

"Until we figure out who the people are that found you, I think you should go radio silent. They offered us a bonus if we found you and brought you to them. It's likely they offered the same deal to the others," Facet said as he nervously drummed his fingers on the table.

"I agree," Venom said.

"But he knows about Lucian. He wanted me to leave. I need to let him know I'm okay, or he may start looking for me," I weakly argued.

"I can help you with that," Facet said.

"Facet, let her reach out. Keep it brief," he said to me.

"Ms. King, we'll do everything in our power to keep you safe, but we need you to work with us," Raptor said.

"Why? Why are you willing to help me? You were paid to find me. I don't understand why you didn't let the other assholes get me. Unless you're holding me for them." Horror filled me at the thought. I could only imagine it was a significant amount of money.

Several of them looked at me like I was out of my fucking mind. Then they glanced to each other as if wondering who was going to tell me.

"Honestly? Part of it is the fact that you're a woman. We don't hurt women. But the biggest reason is Ghost," Venom said as he held my gaze.

"But he hates me," I whispered—the words like a rusty knife to my aching heart.

Facet scoffed, then stood. "You have a lot to learn. Come on, Scarlett. Let's make your call."

The men all stood when I did, but none of them made a move to leave the room except Facet. He held the door open for me, and I stepped around him. When we went past the hall that led to the common area and bar, I stopped in my tracks.

There at the bar was Lucian, and practically draped over him was an attractive blonde who was whispering in his ear. She noticed me standing there and froze as she gazed over his shoulder at me questioningly. Then she must've dismissed me, because she smiled at something he said and threw her head back in a husky laugh.

My chest ached.

"Laila?" Facet asked as he waited for me outside a door down the hall. Lucian's head swiveled, and his blue eyes hit mine. Unable to watch the display any longer, I looked away and picked up the pace to follow Facet into the room he entered.

As he started digging through a drawer, I leaned against the door, closed my eyes, and drew in a ragged breath. I'd known there was the possibility he was with someone, but seeing it firsthand hurt more than I could've imagined.

"Here, this one will work," Facet said as he clicked a battery in place on a cheap cell phone. He held it out to me.

I quickly dialed the number I knew by heart. As it rang, I waited and tried to ignore the tinkling sound of the shards of my heart falling to the floor.

"Who's this?" Ryan's gruff voice growled through the phone.

"It's me, Laila. I can't talk long. I'm safe, but I need some time."

"Yeah, well, your apartment was ransacked, and you weren't answering your phone, messages, or emails. What the fuck, Laila? You scared me to death!"

"Sorry, that's why I'm out of pocket for a bit."

Facet made hurry-up motions.

"I'll be in touch soon," I said, then ended the call and handed the phone to Facet. He quickly disassembled it and tossed most of the pieces in a bin.

"My apartment was ransacked," I whispered as worry hit me for Mrs. Aberdeen and the other tenants.

"How the fuck did he know that already? It's only been hours," Facet said with a frown. His question had me wondering as well. Ryan made it sound like he was on the East Coast.

"Is there a room I can use? I'd really like to get cleaned up," I murmured emotionlessly. I had to shut my feelings down before I fell apart.

"Yeah, I'll take you down there. When you're ready, I'd like to sit down with you and go over what you have. Maybe we could bounce ideas off each other and get farther. Maybe with both of us we could track down the missing girl and figure out this shit with our client. Two heads might be better than one, yeah?" he asked as he gave me a smile.

"Sure," I said with a tight smile. "Facet? Was it you that looked into my real hospital records from after the shooting?"

"No, it wasn't," he said with a concerned frown. "But I'll see what I can find out."

"Thanks," I said, now more worried than I was before. If it wasn't Facet who had found my stuff when he was digging into me, who was it?

Facet was showing me into a room at the end of the hall when I caught motion in my periphery.

Lucian stood there with a hand resting on the wall watching me. His expression was blank, so I had no idea what was going through his head.

He needn't worry about me. As soon as I helped his club with what they needed and ensured no one was after me, I'd be gone.

ELEVEN

Ghost

"BREAK YOUR LITTLE HEART"—ALL TIME LOW

I needed to clear my head after rushing out of church. I knew I'd take an ass-chewing for not only pulling the club into my shit without permission, but for walking out like I did. The thing was, for my own sanity, I had to. During the short time in my room after I'd woken up from Angel's healing, I'd thought maybe we were connecting again—that maybe there was still something there. Voodoo had even said he saw her as my ol' lady. Then she up and asked when she could leave and disappear. It had not only pissed me off, it hurt.

As I sat at the bar with the beer in my hand, Cookie came in the front door.

"Hey, handsome," she said as she stopped next to me and draped an arm around my shoulders. When all I did was grunt, she narrowed her gaze and studied me.

"You okay?" she questioned.

"Honestly, I don't know," I admitted. Cookie may have been one of our strippers and hung out at the clubhouse a lot, but she was also pretty astute. Though I'd fucked her plenty of times, we weren't a thing. She wasn't interested in becoming an ol' lady even if I had wanted her to be. Cookie liked sex, and that was fine with everyone involved. She was also a helluva good woman.

"Aww, you need some tension release?" she teased in my ear as she turned my stool and stepped between my legs. She rested her arms over my shoulders as she looked me in the eye. I dropped my gaze and didn't so much as touch her.

She'd been my go-to for a long time, but my cock didn't give a single twitch at her suggestion. The only woman I could think about was one I couldn't completely reconcile with who she used to be.

"I think my dick is broke. Sorry," I muttered.

She threw her head back and laughed. As she was preparing to push off me, I heard Facet call Laila's name. I glanced over my shoulder to see her cold gaze on me. She quickly looked away and moved down the hall.

"Goddammit," I muttered, knowing damn well what she thought she saw. I carefully set Cookie back so I could stand. She frowned but didn't pout. Instead, she appeared thoughtful.

Though I knew it shouldn't matter what Lila—Laila—thought, it did. With each stride I made that brought me closer to her, I told myself too many years had passed. Too many lies told. Too many things had changed.

It was a bad idea.

I could hear her voice in Facet's room, and I had to force myself to wait in the hall.

Initially, she didn't notice me as they exited his room. As I watched, I hated how close Facet was walking to her. Wanting to rage and greedily scoop her up, I instead bit my tongue and carefully schooled my features. Facet placed a hand at her lower back to guide her, and I had to brace myself on the wall to keep from charging my fucking friend.

The movement caught her attention, and she glanced my way. I stared at her, and though I tried not to allow my eyes to sweep over her, it was a losing battle.

Facet closed the door and gave me a questioning look.

"What's going on in your head?" he asked me.

"Besides wanting to throttle you?" I asked with a cocked brow.

"Huh?" He sounded startled.

I buried my face in my hands and dragged them down over my mouth as I stared at the ceiling. Footsteps sounded above us, and I wondered which prospect was up there. The chapter had grown enough that the rooms downstairs were reserved for patched members and important visitors. Prospects, club girls, and other visitors were upstairs.

"Nothing. Sorry, bro."

"You sure? Come in for a minute," he said as he passed me to open his door.

Reluctantly, I followed him in. Unable to sit still, I paced.

"Jesus, you're making me nervous. What the fuck is your deal? And don't tell me nothing, because I'll call bullshit."

A humorous laugh left my tight chest. To relieve the tension, I rubbed my fist over it, to no avail. When I didn't say anything, Facet did.

"You know a man like Luis Trujillo likely won't forget she witnessed his presence during her family's murder." Facet was clicking and sliding windows around from screen to screen until I was damn near dizzy.

"I pretty much came to the same conclusion."

"So what now? Have you talked to her?"

"A little. I'm not sure I trust myself. I started to lose my shit on her," I admitted, ashamed of how I'd gone off.

"Fucking hell, Ghost. It's not like she was intentionally trying to hurt you or fuck you over. Her family was murdered, she was left for dead, and you were in prison," he said in exasperation as he turned from his screens to stare at me.

"I know. And we weren't exactly together when it happened. I told her to go on with her life when I left for prison. I returned all her letters. We were young. I was sentenced to five years. I didn't want her waiting for me—it wasn't fair. Yet you have no idea how bad it devastated me when I thought she'd died. I don't have the words to describe it." I'd never admit all this shit to any of the other brothers, but Facet was like a vault.

"So you think there's still anything there? Between you two, I mean," he said.

"Hell, I don't know," I said as I dropped my head.

"I think you do," he said, and I hated that he might be right. The Royal Bastards operated on the wrong side of the law, despite the fact that we did it for what we believed were good reasons. As a convicted felon, I could go away for the rest of my life if I was ever caught. The thing is, I believed in the things we did. It wasn't only about the money. It was about the fact that we kept the scales balanced. Maybe we were vigilantes and what we did was legally wrong, but we didn't let people who hurt women, children, and the innocent get away with it.

"The thought of dragging her into this life when she's already dealing with so much doesn't sit right."

"Why don't you let her decide that?"

"So just tell her that 'oh, by the way, we torture and kill people that do the same to others and get away with it?' Because that will go over well, I'm sure." I dropped into the weird round chair he had in his room.

"I didn't say you should start with that, but from what I know about her, she's not exactly an angel either," he said with a cocked brow.

"And that is something I have a hard time reconciling with the girl I once knew," I muttered.

"Well, people change and do what they have to in order to survive. We all cope in different ways. She copes by doing the same thing we do, in a way," he said as he shrugged. He brushed his dark hair out of his eyes. Guy was funny. He was so into his computers that he'd neglect his hair until he couldn't stand it anymore before he got a haircut. Personally, I didn't know why he didn't just grow it out. At least then he could put it up if he needed.

I snorted. "Yeah, okay. You expect me to believe she's a vigilante? You told me she only lurks in the shadows, not the darkness of the web," I said while making sarcastic hand motions.

"Well, she rights wrongs. Same difference," he huffed.

I stared at him.

"What if she won't talk to me?" I asked, realizing I sounded like a damn pussy.

"Jesus Christ, hell must've frozen over, because I've never seen you give a shit if a chick didn't want to give you the time of day." He gave me a crooked grin, and I could tell he was enjoying this. Fucker.

What he didn't understand and I didn't want to admit was that this was different.

Because she mattered.

I'd gone back to my room because I wasn't sure it was a good idea to open myself up if she planned on hauling ass at the first opportunity. Yet after the fifteen-thousandth lap around my room, I couldn't stand it. I stormed to my door and jerked it open. I was startled when a door down the hall flew open at the same time.

"Oh!" she said in surprise, and that simple tiny word had my dick stirring in my jeans. Not wanting her to retreat into her room again, I strode to her doorway.

"Can we talk?" I asked. She appeared hesitant, and I sighed. "Please?"

Her shoulders that she'd held damn near up to her ears slowly fell, and she stepped back to let me in.

The room they'd put her in was like all the rest. Concrete floor, plain comforter on a queen-size bed, nightstand, dresser, desk, and chair. There was a framed image of an old pan-head that one of the original members had taken years ago, but that was it.

She didn't sit, and neither did I. There was too much energy running through me to be still, but for her, I think it was not wanting to feel vulnerable.

"Do you want me to call you Lila or Laila?" I began.

The corner of her mouth quirked up slightly. "Laila. Lila seems like a different life."

"I get that," I said, and I did. "You certainly don't look much like you used to."

Her soft chuckle drew me toward her like a magnet, while I fought the pull. Despite the changes, she was still beautiful. Hell, she might be even more beautiful, if I was being honest. She'd matured into a stunning woman. Her new look suited her, but I wondered if it was really the person she was now, or merely a shell—an armor of sorts.

"What made you get the ink?" I asked her, deciding to start with something neutral.

She sighed and seemed to think about her answer. "I guess because I wanted something that the old me wouldn't have done. In a way, my 'death' became a rebirth."

"The phoenix?" I asked as I shoved my hands in my pockets and my gaze trailed over the colorful edges that peeked above her collar. At some point, she'd changed out of my oversized T-shirt and into a mint-green V-neck. I kind of liked her better in my shirt.

"Actually, no. Not at first. The first one was my dragonfly," she said as she raised her arm and turned it to show me a dragonfly enmeshed with other tattoos on her inner forearm. "The phoenix was my fourth one," she said with a nostalgic, small smile.

"I'm still blown away by all of this, Laila," I muttered, and she pressed her lips flat before inhaling deeply and exhaling slowly.

"Yeah, me too. So do you have any?" she asked as her gaze traced my body hidden by a long-sleeved T-shirt and jeans. It was obvious she never saw my back when they brought me to my room.

"A few," I said and left it at that.

"Is this what it's gonna be like? Chitchatting about our tattoos? Making small talk?" she finally blurted as she took a step toward me. Two lines appeared between her brows as she searched my gaze. Her eyes were the brilliant blue I remembered, and they pulled me in.

Before I realized, I was standing in front of her and feathering my thumb under one eye, then over her brow, ending with the piercing. "You took the contacts out," I murmured softly as my hand swept over the arch of her cheek and I ran her bright pink tresses through my fingers.

"Yes," she whispered as she looked up at me without moving.

"Are you afraid of me?" I asked with a frown as I returned my eyes to hers.

"No," she again whispered.

"Fuck, I'm sorry about everything. Sending your letters back, your parents," I said and took a deep breath to continue with everything I believed I'd done wrong, but she pressed her fingertips over my lips to silence me.

"Don't," she said, and I noticed the shimmer of tears in her blue eyes. Her chest rose and fell rapidly as she tugged her lower lip and piercing with her teeth.

I released her hair, and my hand curled around her throat. The movement when she swallowed rippled against my palm. In slow motion, we grew closer until our lips touched, yet we didn't kiss.

"I missed you so fucking much," she said softly, and the words sent her breath across my lips in a heated caress.

No matter the shitstorm swirling around us, I couldn't stop myself if I tried. My lids lowered, and I stole her breath as my tongue slipped in to twist against hers.

The impact of that kiss rocked me to my core.

TWELVE

Laila

"THE BOTTOM"—DEVOUR THE DAY

I wasn't lying when I told him Lila had died that night. Sometimes, I barely remembered what she was like. Yet the second Lucian kissed me, I was rocketed back to the couple we were all those years ago.

Despite the changes time had wrought in us both, my body simply *knew* his. His taste was like coming home, and the sweep of his tongue against mine set my blood on fire. I'd never stopped loving him, and I knew it, but I'd had no idea how much my body had craved his touch for over eleven years.

In that single scorching kiss, I realized why sex had always been mediocre since him. It was because when you've had the other half of your soul inside you, nothing ever compares.

My fingers clutched his shirt, and a whimper started in my

throat—the place his hand was still locked around as if he owned me.

Evidently, it was enough to break whatever spell had befallen us, because he broke free, and we were left gasping for oxygen. He dipped his head down to rest his forehead on mine.

"I'm sorry, I shouldn't have done that," he said hoarsely.

My brain was so addled that at first, I couldn't form words. Then I remembered the blonde at the bar, and I was mortified. He was with someone, and we'd kissed like we might as well have been fucking. With jerky movements, I stepped back and broke his hold.

"Shit. I'm sorry too. Your…" I wasn't sure what to call her. "Um, she… I…." I stuttered before clearing my throat.

His expression grew confused, then awareness dawned in his eyes. "Laila, Cookie isn't my girl."

"Well, you were certainly cozy, so I'm not sure she sees it that way," I said, unable to keep the snide quality out of my tone. Though I hated to admit it, I was jealous as hell. In my heart, he was mine and always would be. When I hadn't known where he was, it was easier to pretend he was waiting for me somewhere, and as soon as they found my parents' killers, I'd be able to go to him. It was my fairy tale, but it seemed that was all it would ever be.

"Really, she's not," he insisted.

"So, you've never slept with her?" I asked but immediately regretted asking, both because I didn't want to imagine it and because the guilt in his eyes was my answer. The worst part was that it shouldn't matter. He thought I was dead. It had been years. I'd been with other people. It was that stupid fairy tale again.

Wrapping my arms around my middle in defense, I tried to look anywhere but at his haunting blue eyes. "Never mind. That's not my business. Anyway, what did you want to talk about?"

He sighed. "Well, that was a big part of what I wanted to talk about. I know you saw Cookie out there with me, but it wasn't what you thought. I mean, she and I—Fuck, I'm making this worse." He ran a frustrated hand through his dark blond hair, and I wanted to touch it. He'd never had long hair when we were young. Not in a million years would I have thought I'd like it on him—but damn.

"Really, Lucian, you don't owe me an explanation."

"They call me Ghost," he said as he moved closer to me again, and I backed up.

"Ghost? Why?" I asked as I cocked my head, trying to figure out what kind of nickname "Ghost" was for a guy.

He shrugged, suddenly looking uncomfortable. "I, just, um, no one calls me Lucian anymore."

"Okay, so you don't want me to call you Lucian. Check," I said with a definitive nod and pressed my lips flat.

"Goddamn it, that's not what I meant. I—" He stabbed his fingers in his hair and pulled. "Why can't I talk to you without fucking up everything I want to say? We used to be best friends; we were lovers; you were my person. Now, everything is…."

"Fucked?" I offered unhelpfully, and he laughed humorlessly.

"Yeah. That pretty much sums it up. I don't know where we go from here," he said with slumped shoulders.

Pain lanced through my chest, and I smiled sadly. "I think our day in the sun has come and gone. Us together is a dangerous recipe for disaster, Lu—Ghost."

"Bullshit." He frowned and stomped toward me. Stubbornly, I held my ground that time. He pointed a finger at my chest, and I tipped my chin up defiantly. "You don't get to make that decision on your own."

"I can make any fucking decision I want. It may be a fucked-up existence, but it's my motherfucking life, Ghost. So I get to decide what I do." My lip curled as I snarled at him in anger that he dared tell me what I could or couldn't do.

What I wasn't expecting was his hand to shoot out, grab my

hair, and twist slightly as he gripped it in his fist. The motion caused my head to tip back sharply as I stared up at his beautiful flashing eyes. He was only a little over six foot, but to my small frame, he was perfectly massive. The angle made it difficult to swallow, but I stubbornly clenched my jaw, afraid he'd see how he truly affected me.

His nostrils flared as he spoke through clenched teeth. "Well, right now someone is trying to kill you—*again*—and I'm pretty sure I saved your sexy little ass. I think that gives me a little credit."

Biting my tongue, I worked my jaw but didn't reply. The second he called me sexy, I damn near wept. Hell, between my legs, I did. Regardless of all the shit water that had washed under our bridges, my body still craved him as much as it always did. No amount of time or distance was going to change that.

"God, I want to—" He closed his eyes as if he was struggling not to complete the sentence.

"What? What do you want to do, Lucian?" His real name slipped, or maybe it was on purpose; regardless, it had a powerful effect on him.

Jerking me closer, he stared me in the eye and ground out, "I want to fuck the sass right out of you."

Without thought, I boldly said, "Do it."

His eyes widened in surprise.

"I dare you," I angrily whispered.

It was explosive. Like the powerful slam of thunder. We broke.

Hands desperate and clutching, we ripped each other's clothes off. "Holy fucking shit," he said when he saw my pierced nipples. Then he pounced, and I reciprocated.

His mouth was on my neck—kissing, biting, licking. Mine devoured every inch of him I could reach. Teeth scraped skin. Lips sucked on tender flesh. His thick fingers dug into my ass as he lifted me to the desktop, then quickly circled my clit before dipping lower.

He groaned into my shoulder when he encountered my dripping slit that squeezed the two fingers he pressed inside.

"Yes," I moaned as I tangled my hands in the hair I'd been dying to touch, holding his talented lips to my breast. As he sucked on my sensitive nipple, pulling the piercing into his hot mouth, I ground my pussy against the heel of his hand with each curling stroke he made inside me. He gave a satisfied grunt as he suckled, and I chased the orgasm barreling down on me.

"Oh, fuck. Lucian, please. Don't stop!" I begged as I was on the precipice. He continued to work those magic fingers, and I shamelessly used him. When I fell over, I moaned his name like it was the only prayer I knew. His deft hand continued to draw out the life-altering ecstasy as I sucked in ragged breaths.

When the last spasm fluttered, he withdrew, boldly stared into my eyes, and sucked his cream-covered fingers clean. It was the hottest fucking thing I'd ever seen. He clutched behind my knees and jerked me closer to the edge. The movement caused me to fall back, having to brace myself on my hands as he lined up and drove his cock in my weeping pussy.

I gasped in surprise, and my eyes rolled.

"Holy fucking shit," he said as he gritted his teeth and held his breath for a moment. A tiny voice screamed that he was bare in me, but I slapped a hand over it as he gained control and withdrew, only to thrust back home. No one had ever felt that good, but he deserved a warning.

"I swear to Christ, if you give me an STD from some skank, I will cut your dick off and shove it up your ass," I growled out as he stroked long and hard.

A breathless, shocked laugh escaped him as he paused. "I swear on my grandmother's grave, I've never not wrapped my shit. You on the pill?"

"No," I said, and he actually trembled as he appeared to want to cry. I couldn't help but chuckle. "Patch."

"Thank fuck," he said as he began to move again. My legs were thrown over his arms, and his hands held my ass to keep me in place. He seemed to utterly lose control as he fucked me hard and fast. His narrow hips pistoned his thick cock into me, and the desk banged against the wall repeatedly.

Lids heavy and breathless, I watched the animalistic display, barely hanging on to my sanity. It was an absolute mindfuck that I was getting the best dicking of my life from the only man I'd ever loved after he lived years thinking I was dead.

Whether it was that or the fact that together our sexual chemistry was off the charts, I was on the verge of coming again. My gaze dropped to the sight of his slick shaft driving in and out of my greedy pussy, and I lost it.

"Lucian! Fuck, fuck, fuck! Yes, like that! Oh God, yes!" I screamed my praise as my core clenched almost violently around his still thrusting length.

"That's it," he crooned and slowed his movements to draw out the best goddamn orgasm of my life. I shuddered from head to toe as my thighs tried to squeeze him in half. He leaned forward and kissed me with wild abandon until I thought I was going to pass out.

I'd barely re-centered when he resumed his pace.

"This is my goddamn tight pussy, and it always has been. I'm going to fill you full of my cum, and you're going to take every bit," he said as he stared at me through the hair that had fallen across his face. Then he drove me over the edge again as he poured his release into my sweat-soaked body.

Fighting to slow our hearts and breaths, I took a moment to regroup my thoughts. Eyes closed, I tugged on my lip piercing. My eyes popped open when he scooped me up off the hard desk and carried me to the bed, still deeply seated within my sheath.

When he maneuvered us to the bed, he draped his body over mine and kissed me, sucking on my piercing as he released my bottom lip. "This is not over. I thought about taking you to the bathroom to clean up, but I'm only going to get you dirty again," he said in a raspy whisper.

"Oh fuck yes," I sighed. "Dirty me. Please."

He did.

He did.

"Now what?" I asked him three hours and four rounds later. I was a boneless, satiated blob, poured over his hard form. We were soaked in sweat and exhausted.

"I need some time to recoup. Then I can go again," he murmured drowsily, and I couldn't help but laugh—well, as much as my breathlessness allowed.

"I mean about this situation with the people after me. And about us—where do we go from here?"

He wrapped his thick arms around me and squeezed. "Talk later. Sleep now." It was all he mumbled before he was softly snoring.

Snuggling into his incredibly perfect chest, I allowed my mind to shut off long enough to drop into a dreamless sleep.

In his arms, I felt safe for the first time in years.

THIRTEEN

Ghost

"STRANGERS"—THEORY OF A DEADMAN (FEAT. ZERO 9:36)

The soft, warm body curled into mine was a welcome feeling as I pressed my hard length into its softness. I yawned as sleep slowly released me.

"Mmm," she moaned and pushed back into me.

A full tit filled my palm, and the feel of metal had my eyes popping open wide. The sight of hot pink and dark hair in front of me brought back the night before. Every single detail.

Afraid that she wouldn't be as happy about what had happened in the light of day, I held my breath and tried not to move. If she lost her shit, I wanted a few more minutes of her in my arms. Yet, I prayed we were still on the same page.

"Don't tease," she murmured as she wiggled her ass against me, and I couldn't hold in the groan it pulled from the depths of my goddamn soul.

With a stretch, she turned to her back, and I rolled my hips against her side as I buried my nose in her neck. Then I lifted my head to look in her sky-blue eyes.

"Fuck, you have no idea what a beautiful sight you are," I whispered as my heart leaped and fluttered. Honestly, I wasn't completely certain I wasn't dreaming.

She lifted her hand to cradle my cheek. "Do you think we're going to get past everything?"

"It's cute that you think there's an option where we don't," I said in a sleep-raspy voice. "Much as I'd like to fuck you good morning, I'm starving because someone wore my ass out last night. Get up and let's get food."

I rolled out of the bed and pulled on my jeans from the night before. A gasp made me turn. "What?"

She blinked once, then twice before she shook her head.

Shirt, socks, and boots, and I was ready. Meanwhile, she was shuffling around looking for her clothes.

"Where the hell did my bra go?" she muttered and crouched down to look under the bed. "It doesn't just disappear," she said in exasperation before she grabbed another one from her bag.

"You covering those is a crime," I said, and she rolled her eyes.

As I opened the door and waited for her to slip on some slides, I glanced up and held in my laughter.

Her bra was hanging from the ceiling fan.

Thankfully, she didn't notice, and we followed the smell of breakfast cooking. My stomach growled, and I picked up the pace as she giggled.

In no time, we were all sitting at the long table in the club-house kitchen eating breakfast the club girls made. I didn't tell Laila before we left her room, because I wasn't sure how she'd take that, but she seemed okay. Damn, it was strange to think of her as Laila instead of Lila.

Reya and Willow, one of the new girls Cookie had brought in, were cooking that morning. Reya may be a psycho bitch, but she could cook, and she was fun for a crazy fuck. At least she had been. I'd stayed away from her since she tried to tell me she was pregnant and it was mine. All of it turned out to be bullshit. I wanted her kicked out, but Blade had been fucking her by then and stood up for her.

"This is so damn good," Phoenix said as he shoved an entire piece of bacon in his mouth. As he chewed, he reached over and stole one of mine. I tried to stab him with my fork, but I wasn't fast enough. He chuckled with his mouth full.

"Jesus, grow up," grumbled Raptor as he pointed his fork at Phoenix.

Squirrel, Facet, Blade, Sabre, and our newest prospect shuffled in and grabbed plates.

Reya came over with a plate and placed several slices of bacon on Phoenix's plate, all while shoving her tits in his face. "Here you go, baby," she crooned.

Laila made a gagging motion, and Reya shot her a glare. She opened her mouth to run it, and I narrowed my gaze at her. She caught on to my unspoken warning, thank fuck. Then she turned her nose up and sauntered away with an exaggerated shake of her ass.

"Who the hell wears booty shorts and heels to make breakfast?" Laila said with a curled lip. Willow had her back to us as she buttered toast, and her shoulders shook, telling me she'd heard. Unlike Reya, she was dressed in sleeping pants covered in ice-cream cones, a matching tank top, and her red hair messily piled high on her head.

The brothers were in various stages of sitting down at the table when they all paused and looked at Laila, then me. Squirrel had the idiocy to chuckle; the rest wisely kept their mouths shut.

Reya made the rounds with the single guys too, but where Cookie wasn't interested in getting tied down, Reya was itching for it.

Speaking of Cookie—of all the people who could've come to the table, she walked in dressed in a long satin nightgown covered in a diaphanous robe, complete with fine feathers. It was something straight out of a Marilyn Monroe movie, which was likely the look she was going for.

She met my gaze and gave me a mischievous smirk before dropping into Phoenix's lap. "You didn't wake me," she said to Phoenix with a pout of her full lips while her gaze boldly held mine.

Laila stiffened next to me and set her fork down.

"Oh shit," Facet mumbled under his breath next to me.

Before any of us could prepare, Reya came over acting as if she was bringing Phoenix more food. She pretended to trip, and I could see what was about to happen as if it was a movie in my head. Before she spilled a pan full of bacon with sizzling grease down Cookie's arm, Facet and I both jumped up and intercepted the accident about to happen.

"Oh! I'm so sorry! How clumsy of me," Reya said with a surprised expression that I didn't buy for a second. Neither did my brothers, because Raptor stood and gave her a glare.

"Go clean up," he told her in a tone that brooked no argument.

Her jaw ticked, and her ridiculously fake green eyes flashed, but she did as she was told. Laila had worn colored contacts that looked real; Reya's were damn near emerald green. Still, I preferred Laila's natural blue.

"So, who are you, doll?" Cookie asked Laila, and I wanted to grab Laila and run. God deliver me from the cattiness of women.

"Laila," she replied as she rested a possessive hand on my forearm that made my chest swell a little. "And you are?"

"Cookie," she replied with a smile that was blindingly bright as she reached a hand out to shake Laila's.

For a moment, Laila stared at her outstretched hand. When it was on the verge of being uncomfortable, she lifted hers from my arm and gripped Cookie's. "Is your last name Monster?" Laila asked.

Cookie let loose a boisterous laugh and slapped the table. "Holy shit. I never thought I'd see the day," she said when she got her mirth under control.

"The day for what?" Laila asked with a cocked brow and pursed lips. Sass and attitude dripped from her pores.

"It's not important," Cookie said with a surprised grin.

In the background, Reya slammed the refrigerator, then dropped pans in the sink.

"I can get the dishes," Willow quietly offered.

"Good. At least you'll be useful for something," Reya sneered and stomped out of the kitchen. Her footsteps going up the stairs could be heard, followed by the slam of a door.

"I'm talking to Venom about her ass," Raptor said. We all agreed.

Laila got up from the table and brought her dishes to the sink. She said something softly to Willow and began cleaning up with her.

"Raptor, Ghost, Facet—a word," we heard from the doorway. We looked over to our pres. Laila glanced over her shoulder, and I gave her a look asking if she'd be okay. She nodded.

Facet, Raptor, and I followed Venom to his office. He dropped to his chair as if the weight of the world was on his shoulders.

"I got a phone call this morning. Khatri said they received word that we were protecting the hacker that breached their organization."

"Do they know she's here?" I asked as my heart jolted.

"I don't think so, but I'm not sure they'd tell us if they did," Venom replied.

"I'm telling you, they aren't what they are trying to make out," Facet inserted.

"That may be, but do you have proof?" Venom asked as he stroked his close-cropped beard. The man looked tired. With a new baby at home, I imagined he wasn't getting great sleep at night.

"Just that they hired someone else to find Laila too. I also found a multitude of sketchy wire transfers that I'm still tracking. They also have several offshore accounts. I should have something soon," Facet replied in a tone heavy with resignation. He hated it when something eluded him.

"Okay, well that doesn't say anything other than they really wanted to make sure the hacker was found."

"Yeah, but it's who they hired. They hired the Triple X Syndicate. That's who chased and shot you."

"Shit," Raptor muttered.

"So?" I asked, not completely understanding the significance of that.

"So they are brutal and bloodthirsty sociopaths," Facet clarified.

"Some would say that about us," I argued.

"True, but we don't kill for fun or the highest bidder."

"I thought both occupants of the car that chased me died on scene?" I asked with a furrowed brow.

"They did. But that doesn't mean they weren't in contact with others in their crew. What if they saw your plate and passed it on?" Raptor asked.

I snorted. "I'm not stupid. I was using false plates."

"Well, there's that," Venom said with a sigh. "We still haven't discussed the fact that you were stalking your ex who is in WITSEC."

With a chin lift, I crossed my arms. "I was on my own time."

"It was a potentially dangerous situation that you didn't

apprise us of—oh, and with resources Facet provided," Venom deadpanned.

A single shoulder shrug was my reply. He closed his eyes briefly and shook his head.

"In his defense, I had been in contact with her for years before I knew she had a connection to Ghost," Facet said with an apologetic wince.

"I don't even know what the hell to do with you two." Venom palmed his face.

Raptor stifled a snicker, and Venom dropped his hand to glare. Raptor pursed his lips and glanced around innocently.

"For fuck's sake, I feel like a middle school principal," Venom muttered.

"We probably need to turn her over to her handler," Raptor said.

"Hell no!" My words were accompanied by me shooting to my feet.

"Sit. Down!" Venom ground out.

Reluctantly, I did. "I'm not letting her go," I said through gritted teeth. The thought of losing her again nearly unraveled me.

"She's not a fucking stray cat. She has a say in this too. Although being in witness protection, maybe she doesn't. I have no clue," Raptor said with a smirk and a shrug.

"Speaking of, how do we know this isn't connected to why she's in witness protection?" I asked.

"I guess we don't, but I can do more digging," Facet offered. "It seems like it's pretty cut and dry that it's directly from her getting into Khatri's system, but maybe not."

"Well, I'd say no one is really protecting her. To me it seems like they dropped her in WITSEC and then washed their hands of her," I grumbled.

"Okay, so this is the plan," Venom began. "If she's agreeable, which I hope she is, she stays here, where we can do our best to keep her safe. Facet, you do what you do. Find out anything and everything you can about Khatri, Laila's family, and her agent. See if you can find out if there's some kind of connection. If not, we'll have to make a decision on what we're going to do about Khatri, because I need to get back to them by tomorrow."

"I'm on it," Facet said and stood. "Is it okay if I start now?"

"I need something by tonight's church." Venom motioned to the door, and Facet left. I heard him talking to someone, then it was quiet.

"Ghost, you talk to her. If she's not willing to stay here, we can't force her, but you need to make sure she knows she'd be on her own if she left." Venom's gaze leveled on me as he spoke.

I nodded.

"What did you find?" Venom asked Facet without preamble. We'd barely dropped into our seats.

"Well, I think the US Marshals lied to your girl," Facet said as he cast me an uneasy glance. That had me sitting up straight.

"Meaning?" Venom asked.

"The guys who killed her parents are dead. Have been for years."

"What?" I asked. "Maybe they don't know."

Facet shook his head slowly. "They knew."

"How?" Voodoo asked in disbelief.

Then Facet dropped a bomb that left us shell-shocked.

"Because one of their agents hired us—the Ankeny, Iowa, Royal Bastards—to kill them about two months after she went into witness protection. *We* killed them. Rowdy handled it himself."

FOURTEEN

Laila

The door opened, and I pulled my headphones out of my ears and stretched. I'd been doing some research on the computer Facet had cleared for me to use. One of these days I was going to find out who killed my parents. I'd buried myself in the work and had lost track of time. A smile lifted my lips as Lucian stepped through the doorway. He took my breath away, and I needed to be close to him. When he closed the door, I stood and met him halfway.

"Am I going to wake up and find out this was all a dream?" I asked as I wrapped my arms around his waist and looked up at his handsome visage. That's when I realized something was wrong.

His troubled blue eyes stared into mine, and his hands cradled my face. "We need to talk."

"That's never good when said like that," I said cautiously. My gaze bounced from one electric blue eye to the other, seeking a clue as to how bad it was going to be.

"We need you to contact your agent. There are some things we found out that we need to see if he's aware of, but you need to ask them very carefully."

"What are you talking about?"

"The two men who killed your parents are dead."

"But that doesn't make any sense," I argued with a confused, but humorless, laugh. "Maybe your information is wrong."

He sighed heavily. "Trust me, I know."

"Okay. I can reach out to him. He knows I dabble in the dark web a little. I can say I found out they were killed. Would it be best if I try to get him to meet me?" I asked as I tried to swallow, but my throat seemed to have stopped working.

"What's he like?" he asked. "What kind of vibes do you get off him?"

"Honestly? I've never met him in person. My initial case agent retired, and Ryan took over," I explained.

"If he agrees to meet in person, I'll go with you, but he won't know I'm there. If I get any weird feelings, I'm pulling you out."

"Sure," I said.

"There's something else," he hesitantly added.

"There's *more?*" I asked, giving him a *what the fuck* look.

He appeared resigned and briefly rested his forehead against mine. Then he leaned back, and his piercing gaze locked on mine.

"You stumbled into the workings of something bigger than a missing person case. The girl you're looking for is likely involved with the people you inadvertently hacked. We don't know in what capacity. Facet worked his crazy magic and found out they are into some seriously illegal shit. When he started peeling back the layers, it got worse and worse. He thinks they are involved in more than porn and high-end prostitution like they told us." He was holding something back.

"Venom also wants to essentially use you as bait. We think they are part of a human trafficking ring we've been tracking," he said with a clenched jaw. And there it was.

My heart hammered at the thought of people like he was describing getting hold of me. I'd spent damn near half my life hiding from "the bad guys." The thought of being taken out because of my own stupidity really pissed me off.

"What are the odds I wouldn't be safe?" I asked in a tremulous tone.

"I can't say. What I can say is that I will do everything in my power to protect you, and I will not leave your side for a second," he vehemently promised. That was the second time he mentioned being with me during a meeting and then this scheme to get at the shell company I hacked.

"How exactly do you plan on doing that?" I asked in disbelief.

"There's something you don't know," he said with a cagey expression. My eyes narrowed, and I started to pull back, but he gripped my shoulders and held me in place. Mind whirling, I had no idea what he could be talking about, but it didn't sound good.

"What?" I asked in a lower octave.

He sighed. "Don't freak out."

"Saying that is almost guaranteed to make me do exactly that," I deadpanned.

He stepped back and wet his lower lip, then he was gone. Like fucking disappeared.

My chest caved, and I couldn't breathe. "Lucian?" My eyes darted around nervously, and chills skated across my skin.

A touch that ran down my back had me spinning, but there was no one there.

The next one ran down my neck and between my breasts. I shot my hand out to feel for what was causing it but was met with vacant air.

"Lucian!"

A soft chuckle off to my side had me turning again.

"This isn't funny," I said through gritted teeth. "Where did you go?"

A strong grip lifted me by the hips and tossed me on the bed. I tried to scramble off, but I was pushed back, my slides went flying, and my pants were jerked off.

"Lucian!" I demanded, heart pounding. When there was no reply, I shouted, "Ghost!"

"Shhh," I heard whispered as heated breath hit my panties and the feel of his hands slid up my thighs. Teeth bit my clit through the satin, and I couldn't help but suck in a startled breath.

"What the hell is going on?" I demanded.

"I'm going to take you to heaven," Lucian's disembodied voice said before kisses rained over my panties and thighs.

It was the most bizarre experience of my life. I knew his touch, the rate and sound of his breathing, the weight of his body on mine, but I couldn't see him. It should've terrified me, but it was almost like being blindfolded. I never knew what the next move would be, and the anticipation was powerful.

"Holy shit," I whispered when my panties slowly slid down my legs, seemingly under their own power. The heat of his tongue pressing to my slit was startling and damn near made me orgasm immediately.

My leg was thrown over what I could feel as a fabric-covered shoulder, but looked like it was suspended in midair. Then he went to town on my unsuspecting pussy, and my back arched from the bed. I reached up and grabbed the headboard as my eyes slammed shut.

He licked and sucked until I was writhing on the linens. "Oh my God. Holy hell. I'm going to come. Lucian, I'm going to come!"

A soft groan came from where my pussy throbbed and gushed my release. As I lay languid and mindless, I heard a soft rustling before the bed depressed. Then the tickle of his touch raised my shirt and tugged the cups of my bra to expose my breasts. The bed shifted on either side of me, and hot wetness surrounded my nipples one at a time. He flicked the metal of the piercings, and I moaned.

"Lift your legs and hold the back of your knees," he whispered. The air from his breath hit the dampness of my nipples, causing them to pucker tightly.

Unable to think straight, I did as he said.

The heat of his silky-smooth cock prodded at my dripping core before it slowly slid inside, and I gasped. "Oh shit!"

Suddenly he was everywhere. Touching, licking, stroking my sensitive skin. Invisible teeth bit at me teasingly. The silky strands of his hair and his beard tickled over my flesh with each movement. All the while, that magical cock of his stroked my pussy like a goddamn piston.

It was too much and yet not enough. I was overwhelmed with sensation from things I couldn't see or expect. Before I knew it, another orgasm was barreling down on me, and as it got closer, my body seemed to be preparing for the explosion.

"Lucian!" I cried out as utter bliss slammed me into outer space. I was floating and pulsing as stars burst around me. His name was a litany on my lips. Through it all, he never stopped.

When my body began to tremble from the aftershocks, my

eyes slowly fluttered open, and staring down at me was a blue-eyed, dark blond god of a man. He was my first love and more than I could possibly comprehend.

"I love you," I murmured and immediately regretted it when he stopped the movement of his hips and stared at me. His expression was unreadable, and I was afraid I'd messed up. Maybe we weren't there yet. A lot of time had passed. We had grown into different people.

"I never stopped loving you," he admitted, and I wanted to cry. I dropped my legs and wrapped them around his waist.

Fingers curled around biceps, I raised myself to steal a kiss. He began to move again, and I hissed, "Yes!"

"I want you to come again. I want to feel your silky wet pussy tighten and pulse around my cock," he said in a gritty tone against my lips.

His dirty words made my soul weep with need, and I lifted my hips to meet his next thrust. "Oh God, Lucian. Don't you dare stop," I demanded, and he sped up with a wicked grin lighting his face.

Powerful and deep, each stroke drove me closer to what I craved. As my core began to squeeze him, his length seemed to swell until it was too much. My third climax was no less intense than the other two—possibly more so, because with an animalistic grunt, his hot release filled me, and his body shuddered before he dropped to his elbows and buried his face in my neck.

"Fucking hell, that was incredible," he said through ragged breaths, then peppered kisses on my sweat-slick skin.

"Who are *you* telling?" I replied in kind.

As I tried to still my racing heart and gather my breath, I held him close. Afraid he would disappear again, I needed to feel his heated skin against mine.

"How did you do that?" I finally asked.

"Talent," he said with a deep chuckle.

I bumped him with my leg, because he knew that wasn't what I was referring to, though he wasn't lying. The movement caused his cock to partially slip out, and I whimpered in disappointment. He thrust his hips forward, pushing it back in, and I sighed in contentment.

"Madame Laveaux thinks it's because I died after the accident on the way to the hospital but they brought me back. Kip says I was supposed to die. They both think my soul refused to leave my body because it didn't want to leave you." His lips pressed a kiss to my shoulder, sending chills across my body.

"Wait a minute. Kip? As in Kip Harper? But he—"

"Died?" he added when I paused.

"Yeah," I whispered.

He took a deep breath before letting it out in a rush, then he pulled his head back to look at me as he spoke. "He won't leave me. He feels guilty for how my life turned out, and he kind of stuck around."

My eyes went wide before they darted around the room nervously.

He chuckled and shook his head. "He's not here right now."

"Oh, thank God," I said in a relieved exhale. The thought of having an audience was unsettling. The thought of it being a ghostly audience was beyond bizarre.

"And Madame Laveaux?" I asked, trying to keep the jealousy out of my voice as I wondered who she was to him.

Obviously, I didn't do so well, because he grinned knowingly. "She's Voodoo's grandmother. He's one of my brothers in the club. Let's just say she has a bit of a gift. So does Voodoo, but that's another story."

"So you're telling me you're dead?" I swallowed hard at the thought.

"No, not exactly," he hedged.

"What does that even mean?" I asked in exasperation. This was beginning to be too much, and I really thought I might be losing my freaking mind.

"We don't really know," he said with a wince.

I shivered, and chills stole across me again.

FIFTEEN

Ghost

"BRICK"—FROM ASHES TO NEW

"Did you know they make a fucking machine?" Phoenix asked me as we drove to the crime scene in Des Moines. The Royal Bastards operated a legit biohazard cleanup business that specialized in crime and trauma cleanup. It made a good cover for our other business, and there was a crazy amount of money in it.

"I'm sure they make lots of machines." I spoke to him as if he was a child and gawked at him like he was nuts.

He rolled his eyes. "No. I mean a machine that fucks."

"Like an artificial intelligence sex doll?" I asked, confused as to where he was going with this shit.

"No, like a piston machine you can hook a dildo to."

"They do not," Blade piped in from the back.

I scoffed. "You've been hanging around Squirrel too much."

"No, for real. I saw it on the internet. Squirrel's dildo contraption has nothing on it," Phoenix insisted.

"Holy shit. They do!" Blade said as he held his phone up between the seats for us to see.

Phoenix gave it a quick glance before returning his attention to the road. "Told you!"

"I'm ordering it," said Blade with a dark chuckle.

"For what?" I asked with wide-eyed disbelief at what the fuck kind of kink he might be into.

He shrugged. "I bet we can rig something up that works better than Squirrel's dildo rack. Can you imagine if we put a sword at the end or something?"

"Jesus," I muttered as I shook my head. "You need your head read."

Blade shrugged as his eyes stayed glued to his phone he was busy tapping on.

"I told Laila about my gift," I said, changing the subject.

"No shit?" Blade paused to look at me in surprise.

"How did she take it?" Phoenix asked.

"Better than I thought," I said, running a hand through my hair as I looked out the side window. I told them I'd actually showed Laila what I could do. "I also told her that her parents' killers were dead, but I didn't tell her it was our chapter that killed them. It sucks, because Rowdy handled it himself and didn't leave much info behind about it. With him being gone, the answers died with him."

"Damn," he said.

"I know."

"Venom contacted Khatri?" he asked as we took a turn into the older neighborhood. He had been on a job when we finalized all the plans. Venom had told me to give him the rundown today.

"Meet is set for next week. He promised them we had her

locked up in a cell awaiting transport," I said with a curl of my lip. Though it was a lie, the thought alone made me sick.

"And you said we meet with her case agent tomorrow?" Phoenix asked.

"She does," I clarified.

"But we're still gonna be there, right?" Blade's question was surprised.

"Of course."

They both gave relieved sighs.

We pulled up to the address we'd been given by the insurance company and parked the unmarked van in the driveway. Some of the jobs were absolutely disgusting, and I had a strong stomach. This one was particularly bad. It was a murder-suicide in the home of a hoarder.

Evidently, the wife didn't take kindly to her husband starting to throw her things away, because the neighbors said they heard her screaming at him and saw her chasing him to the trash can. They had fought, and she tried to bring things back inside.

He went back in, and she ran after him. The neighbors heard more yelling, then a gunshot, followed shortly by another. It had been all over the news.

Our employees that handled the disposal of the hoarded belongings had already been in, and the dumpster in the driveway was full. It would get hauled off after we finished.

We got out of the vehicle, geared up, and went inside. "Holy mother of God," Phoenix said in a muffled voice behind his mask.

"No shit," I said as the smell hit me.

"Pussies," Blade muttered as he went through the house to the room that was the scene of the crime.

Though the majority of the household goods had been removed, the ones around where the bodies had been were left so we could take care of them. Once we cleaned up the bodily bio scene, the guys could come back in and finish emptying the house. They would do a deep cleaning and then the children of the victims were having a renovation crew come in to remodel the things that weren't salvageable so they could sell the house. The children specifically said they didn't want anything left behind.

"I wouldn't move into this house if someone paid me," Phoenix said as we got to work.

A wave of sadness hit me, and I looked up to see a fuzzy figure of an older man staring at me. He appeared to sigh before he turned to walk off and disappear. I shook it off and got back to the job at hand.

"It's just a house," said Blade. He was a cold fucker.

Though it took a while, we were meticulous, and once satisfied with our results, we packed up. After everything was gathered up, we threw our trash in the dumpster and got back in the van.

"I still have that smell in my nose," Phoenix complained.

"I've told you a million times to put vaporizing rub under your nose," I said with a chuckle. He glared at me.

"I can't. That stuff is gross."

"Then don't bitch about the smell."

"I'm gonna invent something better," he grumbled.

"Okay, sure," I replied with a smirk.

Our next stop was an apartment complex where a party had gotten out of hand and a drunk guy fell over the railing of a fifth-story balcony. That one didn't take as long. We were all glad to be done for the day and headed back to the farm, where we kept the vans parked in an oversized shop.

"You wanna shoot a game of pool after we shower?" Phoenix asked as he pulled on his helmet for the short trip over to the clubhouse.

"I'm game," said Blade.

"Sure. Just let me check on Laila first," I said, then tugged my helmet on too.

"Well, that's gonna be a while," he said with a chuckle before he started his bike. I followed him and Phoenix to the clubhouse, and we parked under the long carport at the end. Those of us who still lived there were allotted a spot to park a vehicle and our bikes. I backed in next to my Challenger with the new rear window Blade helped me replace.

"What was that last comment supposed to mean?" I asked as I hung my helmet on my handlebar.

He and Blade snickered. Then in a falsetto, he screamed, "Oh God, Lucian. Don't you dare stop!"

With a chuckle, I gave him a shove. "Shut the fuck up."

He gave me a shit-eating grin as I shook my head.

"You working at the bike shop tomorrow after the meet with her agent?" Phoenix asked as we approached the door. The cleanup business wasn't a full-time gig for any of us.

"Depends on how things go," I replied. He nodded.

The few members inside gave us a wave or called out as we passed through to the back hall. We split off to our rooms, and I stripped out of my clothes, then cranked the water up. No way was I going to see Laila without washing all that off first. Didn't matter that we garbed up, it still made my skin crawl sometimes. Like the stench of death lingered.

The heat made me flinch initially, but I quickly became accustomed to it and washed my hair, then scrubbed my skin. Once I was clean, I closed my eyes to let the hot water beat over my tired muscles. The shower curtain opened and closed, and I smiled in the knowledge that Laila couldn't resist joining me.

Her hands gripped my hips, and she pressed a kiss to the middle of my back. That gave me pause, as something didn't feel right. The moment it hit me that the kiss hit higher than Laila's small stature would allow, the shower curtain opened again, a gasp could be heard over the water, and I pushed my elbow back and spun.

"Laila!" I shouted as she turned tail and ran. I paused long enough to grab my towel and wrap it around my waist.

"I'll deal with you later!" I snarled at Reya, who gave me a snarky smile.

Dripping water along my path, I rushed to Laila's room and grabbed the knob, only to find it locked. With the side of my fist, I beat on the wood. "Laila! Open up!"

There was no response.

"Goddamn it, Laila! Open the fucking door!"

Brothers began to look out their doors and wander down the hall to see what the commotion was about. Nosy fuckers.

"Good look for you," Phoenix said as he came down the hall, hair still damp from his shower. "What did you do to piss her off this quickly?"

Teeth grinding, I turned to meet the laughing gazes of my brothers. "If someone doesn't get that bitch out of my room and out of this fucking clubhouse for good, I will, and no one will ever find the body."

Their expressions sobered immediately. Venom pushed through the growing crowd. "What the fuck is going on? I could hear you down in my office," he said with a frown.

"Phoenix, Blade, and I just finished the cleanup jobs, and I went to take a shower. Fucking Reya came in behind me, and I thought it was Laila. Then for some goddamn unlucky reason, Laila came walking into the bathroom and found us in the shower together before I could do anything," I spat the explanation out with a glare.

Venom motioned to Phoenix. "Get her out of here."

Phoenix nodded and went into my room, where yelling ensued.

"Get some goddamn clothes on, and give her time to calm down," Venom said practically.

I stormed back to my room to find Phoenix standing there with his arms crossed while Reya took her time dressing.

"You are lucky I don't wring your scrawny neck," I said to her before grabbing clean clothes and slamming my bathroom door. Angrily, I dried off and dressed. By the time I finished, Phoenix and Reya had vacated my room.

Taking several deep breaths to calm myself down, I went back to Laila's door. Fighting the urge to bang on the door again, I knocked lightly. "Laila, baby, open up. Please?"

Silence.

Closing my eyes, I rested my head on the wood. "Laila, please," I begged.

Shock hit me when the door suddenly opened, and I stumbled, nearly falling into the room.

"Laila, I swear it wasn't what you think," I began.

She snorted. "Why is it that every guy says that when they fuck up?"

"But I didn't, I swear to you," I promised.

She pursed her lips as she held the door so I couldn't advance further in the room. The scent of her perfume or body spray hit me, and my fucking knees went weak. Finally, she stepped back and let me in.

"I believe you," she said.

"You do?" I asked in disbelief.

"Yes. Because I doubt you would've sent someone to tell me to join you in the shower if you were planning on messing with someone in there." She crossed her arms.

I frowned. "Who told you to come to my shower?"

"That Willow girl. I'm a little surprised, because she seemed nice the day we cleaned up together. I guess it goes to prove you can't trust people," she huffed.

"Wait. You're saying Willow told you to go to my room? Exactly what did she say?" I was ready to kick Willow's ass to the curb too. I was pissed at Cookie for bringing her in.

"She knocked on the door and said you wanted me to join you in the shower. I actually laughed and was just going to watch you, but I got a little more than I bargained for. I now regret that I didn't drag her out of there by the hair like I wanted to," she said with a cocked brow.

"I wish you had," I grumbled.

"No, you don't, because after I had whooped her ass, I would've gone after you. So you're lucky I had time to cool down." She shot me a smirk, and relief caused my shoulders to droop.

"Move your shit into my room," I said without stopping to think.

Her eyes popped wide. "What?"

"You heard me. I don't know why I didn't have you do it immediately. If you'd been in there, none of this would've happened," I said as I damn near pouted. *What the hell is happening to me?*

A brilliant smile lit her face before she tugged that piercing with her teeth. "You want me in your room?"

I boldly stepped closer and wrapped her in my arms. The feel of her soft curves against the planes of my body was heavenly. I was pretty sure I could hold her all day, every day, and never get tired of the feeling.

"Yeah. As a matter of fact, after we get this shit all sorted, I want to look for a house we can move into," I admitted.

Her gaze became wary. "You want us to get a *house* together?"

"Laila, what part of 'you're mine,' or 'I love you,' or 'I'm never letting you go again' did you not understand?"

"None of it, but are you sure it's not too sudden?"

"Absolutely not. You've been mine since you were eight years old. We've already lost and wasted too much time. If there is anything I've learned, it's that life is too fucking short. When you find that special person, you hang on and never let go. I thought I lost you once, Laila-Lila. I'm not doing it again."

She rested her cheek against my chest and hugged my waist tight. "I love you," she said against my shirt. The last of my anger at Reya and the position she'd put me in dissolved in the feel and scent of the woman in my arms.

I kissed the crown of her head. "I love you too."

SIXTEEN

Laila

"WHO MADE WHO"—AC/DC

I'd changed a lot over the years. I'd been a fairly sweet person as a kid, but everything I'd been through had hardened me. That was probably why when I walked in and saw that snarky bitch in the shower with my man, I'd been torn in my response.

Laila—the me I was now—wanted to drag her out of the shower and beat the ever-loving dog snot out of her. Lila—the me that was buried deep inside—reacted with a heart-dropping pain and ran. It didn't take me long to figure out that there was no way he'd asked me to join him knowing he'd be in there with someone else.

They had called Willow back to the clubhouse because she was gone when Ghost went looking for her. I was glad I was allowed to be there when she was confronted. The poor girl looked terrified, and I tried to be a reassuring presence.

"Tell us exactly what happened," Venom said in a calm, fatherly tone.

Her nervous gaze darted around to each occupant of the room before settling on mine. "I'm so sorry." Then she gave Venom her attention. "I didn't think. I knew Ghost and Laila were together, so it didn't seem out of the ordinary that he would want her to join him in the shower." Her cheeks burned red.

"But we know he didn't send you for Laila, so who did and what was said?" Venom continued.

"I was getting ready to leave for work, and Reya told me she needed to get supper started. She asked if I could relay the message on my way out. I didn't think it was a big deal. I thought it was sweet. If I'd known, I never would've done it. Again, I'm so sorry," she said with tears shimmering in her eyes.

"Okay, thank you, Willow," Venom said.

"Can I go back to work?" she asked in a small voice as she twisted her purse handle.

"Yes, Facet will give you a ride back," Venom said as he tapped his fingers in agitation on the table.

I didn't think her face could get any redder, but hell if it didn't. Her creamy complexion flamed as she nodded but dropped her gaze to the floor.

Facet stood, and she followed him out of the room.

"Where did Reya go?" Venom asked.

"I tossed her out the door," Phoenix said unapologetically with a casual shrug. Voodoo and Angel snickered.

"You already know we never liked her," Voodoo said, giving a head nod toward Angel.

"Good. No one lets her back in. She's out, and I don't wanna see her here again," Venom said with a frown.

"I still don't understand why she would do that. From what I've seen, Ghost never gave her reason to believe he wanted her, so what did she have to gain by hurting me?" I asked, truly confused by her hateful behavior. Hell, the woman didn't know me.

Ghost snorted in disgust. "I can tell you why—to get even with me, that's why. She tried to trap me once, and I not only denied her, I embarrassed her. Personally, I think she finally had something she thought she could fuck me over with."

"How could she think she'd get away with that, though? Even if I had believed it and hated you, or left, did she think you would forgive her for that?" I was truly trying to figure out why someone could be so spiteful.

"Because she's batshit crazy, that's why. I doubt she had a concrete grasp on how it would play out in the long run. In her eyes, if she caused Ghost pain and sadness then she won. At least that's what I think, for what it's worth," Voodoo said as he used a sharp-looking silver dagger to clean under his fingernails.

"What I want to know is, who the hell is gonna cook?" Blade grumbled.

"I can do it," I offered.

"Hell, no," Ghost snapped. Chains cast him a side-eye like he was waiting for me to kick his ass for being a bossy dick.

I was on the verge of telling him to kiss my ass when he added, "The club girls usually do that. I'm not having anyone thinking you're a club girl. They haven't been claimed by anyone."

I mouthed an "oh." Then I wanted to ask what I was to him exactly, but that could wait until we were alone.

"Actually, it's not a problem. Grams has been on my ass to let her do the cooking, but there was no way I was having her in here with Reya. Not that she doesn't have an idea of some of the things that happen here, but, Reya was a bitch, and I wasn't going to put up with her talking shit to Grams." Venom ran a hand down his face.

"Fucking women," Phoenix said. "No offense," he said to me, causing me to laugh.

"None taken," I said with a suppressed grin because Reya *had* been a bitch. "I just don't understand why you all kept her around so long if she was that big of a troublemaker."

Several of the guys looked uncomfortable, but none answered me. I could guess what that meant. When no one had anything else to add, Venom sighed and leaned back in his chair. "Fine. Now that that's all settled, can I go home to my woman?" he asked with a cocked brow.

"We're good," Ghost said.

"Ghost, Blade, Phoenix, and Chains, get to bed at a decent time. I want you on your A-game when Laila meets with her case agent in the morning," he said as he stood. They all nodded.

The guys dispersed, and Chains went out the front door with Venom, followed by Voodoo and Angel. They all lived outside of the compound with their families. I glanced at Ghost as we made our way back to his room. That would be us one day, I thought with a smile.

Ghost hadn't waited a minute after I agreed to move my meager belongings over to his room. Hand in hand, we went in, and he closed and locked the door.

"You sure you're going to be okay meeting with Ryan tomorrow?" he asked me as he turned to pull me into his arms.

With a roll of my eyes, I pressed my palms to his firm chest. It wasn't like I was going alone. My car was parked at one of their shops, but we discussed it and decided they would drive in case things went unexpectedly.

I stood on my tiptoes and pressed a kiss to his perfect lips. His facial hair tickled, and I caressed the side of his nose with mine. "I'll be fine, and you and the boys will be right there. Now what do you say we go to bed?"

A sly grin lifted his lips. "That sounds absolutely amazing."

"Don't pull your disappearing act on me though. It was hot, but I want to be able to see you," I said as I wagged a finger at him.

He barked out a laugh, and we went to bed. Of course, there was no sleeping for some time.

When I arrived at the designated location, I'd gone to the counter and ordered a chocolate donut with coconut flakes on it and a black coffee. God knew after my lack of sleep the night before, I needed the caffeine.

"Ryan?" I asked as I stepped up to the corner table in the donut shop where we'd agreed to meet. He was nothing like I'd expected, but he was wearing a red collared shirt and a black ball cap like he'd said. He sipped from his cup as he watched me over the rim.

"I told you not to bring anyone," he said.

Startled, I did my best to hide it. Nervously, I glanced to my side where I assumed Ghost was standing. No way could he see him.

"I didn't," I said cautiously with a narrowed gaze.

He snorted. "Okay, and the guy watching us from the bookstore across the street?"

Refusing to look, I shrugged. "I have no clue what you're talking about." Though we both knew Phoenix was over there and Chains was right outside the front door, out of sight and reading a newspaper.

He shook his head. "Sit down."

As I did as he said, I studied him. He was younger than I thought—probably not much older than me. He had a close-cropped goatee, and his dark hair seemed short and neat. He was rugged but seemed out of place in the preppy red polo shirt.

"What did you find out that was so important I meet with you in person? Do you know how expensive last-minute flights are?" With a cocked brow, he took another sip of his coffee, then picked up the glazed donut and took a bite. As he chewed, he patiently waited for me to talk.

A quick glance around showed no one was close by or paying us any attention. I took the lid off my cup and added a generous amount of sugar and creamer to it. "The two men who killed my parents are dead," I softly announced as I stirred my coffee and watched for his reaction.

He didn't so much as bat an eye.

"Are you surprised?" I asked. "Because you don't seem like you are."

"Maybe I am surprised but know better than to let anyone read my thoughts through my expression."

I snorted in disbelief, and he calmly watched me as he took another sip of his coffee.

"So are you going to tell me why I'm still in witness protection?" Anger simmered in my blood as I stared him down, waiting for his reply. "Or do I need to have my friends look into you and what the fuck you've been pulling."

Briefly he closed his eyes before he opened them and damn near stared into my soul with his hazel gaze.

"We might need to go somewhere else for this conversation," he said softly as he leaned slightly across the table. There was a subtle squeeze on the back of my neck.

"No, I think I like where we are just fine, thank you," I said, letting my South Carolina accent slip through.

His knee bounced under the table, and his fingers tapped on the surface as he debated what his next move would be. For someone who said he didn't like to let people read him, his agitation was hitting me in waves.

When I thought he was going to blow me off, he shocked the shit out of me.

Another quick glance around the shop, and he spun his paper cup in slow circles on the table. "Your previous agent?"

"Carl," I offered, and he nodded.

"He didn't retire. The agency wasn't going to tell you he was killed. The thing is, he saw it coming. Something had spooked him. He reached out to me and asked me to do what I had to in order to get your case if anything happened to him. Made me promise not to let anything happen to you."

"If he didn't trust the agency, why would he trust you? Who were you to him?"

"Because Carl and I had a history prior to the US Marshals. Carl was my team leader. We were in the Marine Raider Regiment together. Well, it was the Marine Special Operations Regiment when we first met. I was a young kid then, fresh out of training. He took me in and was more of a father figure than I'd ever had. He never crossed the line or showed favoritism as my NCO, but he molded me into the man I am today. I have him to thank for everything. I've been busting my ass to find the people responsible for taking his life," he said as he lifted the hat, ran a hand through his hair, then replaced the cap.

"So someone in the US Marshals had him killed?" I asked in disbelief.

"That's what I believe. Someone in the US Marshals betrayed Carl and was likely on Luis's payroll. We think that was how he got out of the country so easily after he had your family killed. Anyway, I think it was pure coincidence that he found out you were still alive, but he didn't have time to access your new identity before he told Luis." He rasped a hand over the whiskers on his face. "I'm pretty sure Luis killed Carl—but not before he gave me all your files and wiped his computer."

"Then shouldn't I be safe from Luis. Right?"

"Not exactly."

"What do you mean... not exactly?"

"For about four years before your father's death, he was working with someone in the FBI to uncover a powerful group involved in drug and human trafficking. I have no idea the exact connection or what he was doing because all of his files disappeared the night he died."

Despite the years, I winced at mention of my father's death. Then I looked him in the eye. "I'm still confused. Why would that put me in danger?"

His gaze burning into mine, he quietly said, "Because your parents lied about your mother's pregnancy and passed you off as theirs, and your real father is Luis Trujillo."

The faint sound of a sharp inhale was thankfully disrupted by one of the cashiers dropping a pot of coffee on the floor behind the counter. Still, I sat in stunned silence.

"Excuse me?" I finally choked out. No way was Luis Trujillo, leader of the most ruthless cartel of modern time, my father.

"Carl believed that when your 'adopted' father started helping the FBI, Luis was gunning for him because he had a hand in the drug trafficking, if not the human trafficking as well. He also believed that Luis didn't realize you were his child—until he stole your father's files."

"Shit. Then my dad knew Luis was my... biological father?" I asked as panic began to skate through my veins and seize my heart.

"We believe that was part of his driving force behind taking Luis down."

"But then who is my mother?" I asked, almost afraid to hear the answer.

He took a deep breath before inflating his cheeks and huffing out. "Priscilla Kellerman."

"But… that's… that's my aunt. That's impossible. She died before I was born!"

"Not exactly," Ryan said hesitantly.

"What do you mean, *not exactly?*" Exasperation was leaking into my voice.

"Your mother and father helped her hide herself and her pregnancy, faked your mother's pregnancy, then passed you off as their child. They found a midwife willing to do an in-home delivery and keep quiet about who actually gave birth to you. Everything was buried." He appeared resigned, maybe even apologetic. It suddenly made sense why my parents always said I looked so much like my aunt. I assumed it was simply family connection.

"Because Luis was my father?" I asked, already piecing it together.

"Yes. I guess she had a brief affair with him until she found out he was married. She left him, and he lost his shit and looked for her. Carl was pretty sure Luis didn't know she was pregnant when she left."

"Because he didn't want Luis to find me," I murmured, still in shock.

"Exactly. Luis Trujillo is likely the most vicious cartel boss of our time."

SEVENTEEN

Ghost

"PAPERCUT"—LINKIN PARK

As I stood there listening to the conversation unfold between Laila and who she'd thought was her case agent, I was blown away. Likely not as blown away as she was, finding out her entire life was a lie.

Since entering witness protection, her life became the lie that she told on her terms. Now she had been told that every day before that was too. Except not all of it. Regardless of who she really was, I had always loved her and so had her parents.

"But what are the odds that he'd find me and find out I was his daughter? Surely it's not on his radar after this many years. I'm a grown woman. Why would he have any interest in me?" she asked.

"Because if he found out he had a child and that she was kept from him, he'd see that as an affront to him personally and as theft of something that belongs to him," Ryan tried to explain. He set his cup down and palmed his hands on the table.

"I'm not an object to be owned! I'm a human, and if I lived my entire life without him and vice versa, why would it matter?" She was exasperated, but she didn't have a clue what kind of person Luis Trujillo was.

"Luis is certifiable, that's why it would matter. I think staying here is a mistake. It's a matter of time before Luis finds out about you, if he hasn't already. You need to come with me. Laila, I can keep you safe. Those thug bikers you're staying with won't be able to do that—not like I can. This is my job. We need to leave now. I rented a car to go back in, unless you'd rather fly," he said as he reached across the table and rested a hand over hers.

And that was enough of that conversation. Using a single finger, I leaned over the table and pushed his coffee cup into his lap. Grim satisfaction filled me at his squeal when the hot liquid hit what I hoped was his dick.

While he was trying to clean up the mess, I grabbed Laila's arm and lifted her from her chair. I whispered in her ear, "Tell him you'll be in touch."

"I'll be in touch!" she said over her shoulder with a wave as I rushed her out of the donut shop, pushing through the short line of people. The door nearly shattered with the force of my hand shoving it open.

"Whoa! What's going on?" Chains asked as he ditched the paper and followed us.

"If he follows, stop him. Whatever it takes," I ground out. Chains immediately nodded and placed his hand on the gun I knew he had in the back of his pants.

"Ghost! Stop! You're acting like a nutcase! Chains, don't you dare shoot him. He is a good guy." She glowered at Chains as I rushed her around the corner and into the blacked-out SUV we had waiting.

"Good guy, my ass," I muttered and shut the door behind us. Then I told Blade, "Let's go."

Without hesitation, he pulled away and headed back to the clubhouse.

"Why did you do that?" Laila turned sideways in her seat to glare at me. Her eyes flashed fire, and she crossed her arms belligerently, but I wasn't intimidated.

"He knows nothing about us if he could sit there and tell you we couldn't keep you safe. What I want to know is how the hell he knew you were with us to begin with. Did you tell him?" I asked accusingly.

Her eyes widened, and if it could, steam would've shot out of her ears. "Don't be an asshole! If I'd told him where I was, don't you think Facet would've known? He was right there when I called him. Both times!"

I pulled out my phone and hit send on the number I needed.

"Did it all go well?" Venom asked.

"Yes and no. Can you have Sabre check Laila's apartment? I think there was surveillance on it." Laila gasped, and her eyes went wide.

"He's on a cleaning job with Squirrel, but I'll get someone on it. You headed back now?" Venom asked.

"Yes."

"Good. See you when you get here." The line went dead, and I lifted one ass cheek to shove my phone in my back pocket. Venom would expect a full report on what had transpired. He was gonna shit when I told him everything.

"You think my apartment was being watched? By who? Ryan or the other people hired to find me?" she demanded.

"Don't know, but we're gonna find out. How did Ryan know

your apartment had been tossed hours after we left? How did he know you were with us?" I could tell by the look in her eyes that these were questions she'd already asked herself. For all I knew, her biological sperm donor could've done it, but I didn't want to toss that out to give her one more thing to worry about.

And that....

Jesus fucking Christ, I never would've thought her parents had lied about her birth. Her aunt had only been mentioned a handful of times in all the years I'd been part of her family. Not that her aunt had been a secret, but she died before Lila was born. Or so we thought.

Then her being Luis Trujillo's daughter? Holy fuck.

Her brave, bold facade seemed to wilt in front of my eyes as the events of the day seemed to sink in. With a firm grip around the back of her neck, I pulled her close until our foreheads and noses touched.

"It's going to be okay. We're going to figure this out," I promised her, hoping I wasn't telling her lies.

She buried her face in my neck, and my eyes met Blade's in the rearview. He was obviously thinking the same thing I was—this was an absolute clusterfuck.

The remainder of the trip back to the clubhouse was quiet, and I knew she was stewing on everything she'd learned.

Korrie, Loralei, and Jasmine were in the kitchen when we got back. They were making a birthday cake for Kira. I brought Laila in and asked if she wanted to hang with the girls or lie down for a bit. She'd had a lot thrown at her today.

"I'd rather not be alone. I'll think too much," she said, swallowing hard.

Enveloping her in my arms, I held her close. She seemed too fucking breakable in that moment, and I hated it. Though I happily would've held her all day, I looked up over her shoulder and saw Venom motioning with his head to his office.

I hated to leave her, but I leaned back and framed her face with my hands. "I'll try to keep this short, then I'll come get you."

She nodded, and we entered the kitchen. I made introductions. The girls called out greetings with wide smiles. It was obvious my brothers had been talking to their ol' ladies, because none of them seemed surprised.

"I love your hair," I heard Loralei say to her as I turned to report to my president's office. Knowing she was in good hands, I breathed a little easier.

As I hit the hall entry that led to Venom's office, I heard the front door open. Glancing over my shoulder, I saw Chains and Phoenix come in. I waved them to follow.

Blade and Raptor were already waiting when we went in and closed the door. It wasn't a huge room, and they were in the few chairs, so we stood.

When I filled everyone in, there was more than one expression of disbelief. Venom was, as usual, stoic as he took in every word.

"So you're telling me her father is Luis fucking Trujillo?" Blade asked with a wide-eyed stare that I rarely saw.

"Yeah. At least according to her case agent. Crazy shit, huh?" I asked as I raked a hand through my hair and then covered my mouth to hold back my frustrated shout.

Blade seemed to go pale as he fell back in his chair.

"Dude, you okay?" Chains asked as we all studied our usually unflappable brother curiously.

"No. This is bad. So fucking bad," he said as he bolted from his chair and paced the small room with his jaw muscle jumping and his hands clenched.

"Blade, what the actual fuck?" Raptor asked.

"You know I'm solid as fuck. I can handle a lot. You have

always had my back, but if we're going up against Luis, we're stepping into a pile of shit we are not prepared for," he said before he stopped and dropped his hands to his knees and breathed deeply.

"What do you know?" Venom asked as he narrowed his eyes.

Blade stood, ripped his shirt off, and turned. "That's what I know. That's how Luis deals with people who disagree with him."

His muscular back was a mess of crisscrossing scars.

"What the fuck?" I asked, stunned. He quickly pulled his shirt back on and met my gaze.

"I stepped in when he was going to whip a nine-year-old boy. Instead, he used me and made the boy watch." His lip curled in a snarl. "If you think I'm fucked in the head and heartless, you have another thing coming. Because that man is who made me what I am, and he's ten times worse."

Blade's revelation shook me—and I'm pretty sure every brother in the room. We agreed to look into Laila's paternity and make a decision about what to do with Luis after we dealt with Khatri. One fire at a time.

We settled on a plan. With the meet set for early next week, we had a little time to prepare and ground ourselves. At that moment, I needed Laila. I made a beeline to the kitchen.

Women's laughter filtered through the common area, and it was strange to think this was a mens' clubhouse. When I stopped in the doorway, I saw Laila and the other girls watching Loralei put the finishing touches on Kira's cake.

She looked up, and a soft smile curved her lips. As if she could read my mind and the restless need I had brewing in my veins, she said a few soft words to the other ol' ladies, who shot knowing smiles in my direction, then went back to what they were doing.

"You wanna go talk at the bar or in the room?" she asked as she rested her palms on my chest. I gripped her wrists, holding her against me.

"Room," I said abruptly. Her sky-blue eyes searched my face before she nodded and twisted her arms in my grip to curl her hands with mine and lace our fingers.

I wanted to toss her over my shoulder caveman style, but I didn't. Instead, I practically dragged her down the hall and into our room.

I flipped the lock, having learned my lesson with that shit, and advanced on her. A heated look turned her eyes to blue flame. Her tongue wet her bottom lip, and I ripped off my shirt and went for my pants.

"You like those clothes?" I asked as my buckle clanked.

"Yes, why?" she asked with a confused wrinkle to her brow.

"Then you better take them off before I get to them." My boots got kicked off and my jeans hit the floor.

Her eyes went wide as she stalled, then her hands were a blur as she stripped to her socks. I wanted to chuckle at the rubber ducks on them, but she quickly toed them off and stepped toward me, and they were the last thing on my mind. By then I was solely focused on losing myself in her and taking away her worries for the time it took to wear ourselves out.

Her dainty hands explored my chest and up to my shoulders as I palmed her ass and lifted her. She wrapped her legs tightly around my waist, and I sat on the edge of the bed.

"What do you want?" she asked softly.

A half smile kicked up the corner of my mouth as I shook my head slightly. "You" was my answer before I slid one hand to her smooth back and the other cupped the back of her neck.

Our lips crashed together like thunder, and our tongues lashed as our teeth clicked in a savage and needy kiss. Her slick pussy slid over my hard shaft, and I broke from her lips to graze her neck with my teeth before I gave her a bite that I soothed with my tongue.

"I need to be inside you," I said against her skin as my fingers threaded through her colorful hair and gripped tightly.

"Yes," she hissed as she rose and wrapped her soft hand around my cock. She circled the tip at her entrance until I was as soaked as she was. Then she lowered herself in increments until she sat flush on my hips.

It was fucking heaven. For a moment we didn't move. We simply held each other as the profound feeling of being whole washed over us. I savored the feel of my thick length sheathed in her tight, wet heat. My face pressed to her neck, my arms wrapped around her tightly, and I clung to her like a man drowning.

None of the shit from the past existed in those moments. Nor did any of the swirling trouble brewing. Only me and her. The only noises were our ragged breaths, the pounding of my heart, and the muted sounds coming from down the hall.

When she lifted herself, I wanted to groan at the perfect sensation of the wet slide of skin on skin. She squeezed her fucking pussy around my cock as she dropped back down, and I did.

"Fuck, yes," I rasped as I reveled in the soft feel of her decorated skin under my fingertips. "Ride me, baby."

She splayed her hands over my chest and moved them to hold on to my shoulders. Slowly, she lifted and then sensually moved over me as I let go and leaned back on my hands. Though I wanted nothing more than to grip her hips and slam her down on my cock until I couldn't see straight, I knew she needed to feel in control. After getting blindsided by everything today, she could do what she wanted to me, and I'd let her.

As she used my body for balance, I scooted us back further on the bed until I could lie down. Her angle changed when she leaned onto my chest, and I sucked a sharp breath in.

"Feel good?" she asked in a breathy voice as she continued the slow torture of the best kind.

"No," I croaked as I fought coming too soon.

She paused, and for a moment, hurt flashed in her expressive eyes.

A devious grin spread over my face. "You feel better than good. You feel like perfection, and each time is better than the last."

A smirk crossed her face before I thrust my hips up and hit that spot that made her eyes roll. Then her mouth went lax as her back arched.

"You still want to go at your pace?" I asked as I lifted my shoulders from the bed and circled one pierced nipple with my tongue.

"Fuck," she breathed when I repeated the motion on the other side. My teeth tugged gently before I sucked on her and encouraged her to move with a slight rotation of my hips.

When she began to move and grind, I lay back and watched her chase her orgasm. She was beautiful, all sleek lines and colorful ink. Flashes of metal that teased and taunted. Long hair that tickled my thighs and balls when she threw her head back. Every little thing about her was stunning. She was a goddess on Earth, but she was my goddess.

Her movements sped up, and her breathing came in short gasps.

"That's it, baby, get there." I crooned the encouraging words as I raised one hand to slip between us until my thumb found her clit that she'd been working over. Pressure and a pinch, then several hard circles, and she exploded.

"Oh God," she ground out between clenched teeth as her sweet, hot cunt pulsed around me and I drove up into the heaven of her body. When she seemed to come down from her high, followed by a residual shudder, I lifted her off and flipped around.

Facedown and in a postorgasmic haze, she sprawled on the

bedding. I lifted her hips, exposing her glistening pussy. Unable to stop myself, I leaned over to swipe my tongue through her soaking slit, gathering her creamy cum one lick at a time.

"Fuck, you taste incredible," I said before nipping the perfect, full globe of her ass. She gave a satisfied groan, and I smiled. Then I closed her legs, straddled her calves, and lined myself up.

"Hang on, because you're in for the ride of your life, Laila," I said as I plunged to the base into her dripping wet sheath. She squeezed her inner muscles so tight, it was like a fist gripping me, and I stuttered on my next stroke. "Goddamn."

"Don't stop. You promised the ride of my life," she said between ragged breaths.

My reply was to withdraw, then thrust hard and deep. Lost in the perfection that was consuming me, I repeated the motion over and over. Sweat ran down my chest and back—it dripped in my eyes, and my hair stuck to my face.

Her skin was slick, and my grip slipped but recovered. With each snap of my hips, she pushed back into me, giving as good as she got. I watched as one hand released the covers, and she reached down to feel my shaft slamming into her core. I knew her fingers were strumming her clit, and it sent me over the edge.

The telltale tingle began that shot down my spine, and my fucking nuts pulled up tight as my cock swelled. A growl rumbled deep in my chest as my release drew closer. White explosions of light flashed on the edge of my vision.

"Fuck, yes!" I shouted when I closed my eyes and blew my load deep in her tight pussy. With each throb of my cock as my cum continued to fill her, her slick walls pulsed and fluttered around me.

I released her hips to smooth my hands down her back, admiring the inked surface. She looked nothing like I imagined Lila would've grown up to be, but maybe she was right—Lila was gone. Or maybe Lila's death was a rebirth for Laila. Lila's sweet soul was still in there, she had just been finding herself and unfurling her wings.

When I traced the valley of her spine, goose bumps broke out over her colorful skin, and she shivered. Entranced, I continued to glide over her body, appreciating the changes and the beautiful work of art that was my woman.

"I meant it when I said I love you," I said.

She moved her head to look over her shoulder. As it always did, the incredible blue of her eyes took my breath away. "I never thought I'd see you again. I had no idea you'd left South Carolina, because I avoided looking you up. I was afraid to see how you'd moved on. I never stopped loving you," she said as her unwavering gaze held mine.

"I also meant it when I said you were mine. I'm not letting you go."

Something that looked suspiciously like regret flickered in her eyes. It told me that she still didn't believe we'd find a way through this. Not wanting to dwell on the negative shit, I left her body but pulled her into my arms. Spooning her into my front, I swept her hair up out of my way and held her with my lips absently rubbing over her neck, her ear, and her jaw.

She twisted in my arms to face me. One soft hand cradled my cheek, her fingers stroking my short beard.

"Tell me about your tattoo," she said with a serene smile that told me she was also stealing this time for us.

A sad laugh slipped from my throat before I could tamp it down. "I think it's pretty self-explanatory."

"When did you have it done?" she prodded.

Pressing my lips tight as I rolled them between my teeth, I gazed at the ceiling. "A guy started it when I was in prison. Then I had it finished after I got paroled."

Gently, she nudged me to turn to my stomach. I complied and

used my folded arms as a pillow. Her fingers trailed over the lines, and I knew what she was seeing. There was no color, because at that time in my life I felt as if all the color had been sucked from the world. She traced the reaper swinging his scythe in a wide sweep through the night sky. The stars plummeted as he ruthlessly cut them down. Below, on the ground, was an angel gathering them as they fell.

"It's achingly beautiful." I heard the unspoken "but" in her tone.

I waited to see if she'd finish her thought.

"I think you should add to it."

Lifting my head, I looked at her with a confused half smile. "What should I add?"

"Someone putting the stars back in the sky," she replied with the slightest lift of the corners of her mouth.

With a chuckle, I rolled to rest on one elbow. "Then I think we need to find a place for an addition to your ink as well."

"Oh really," she drew out. "And what do I need?"

"Something that says you're mine."

She laughed, and I grinned. "I'm not kidding."

"You mean like one of those *Property of* type tattoos?" she asked with amused incredulity.

"Yeah. Something like that."

"Hmm, we'll see," she said with a twinkle in her eyes.

I gave a playful growl and pounced on her. Her giggles rang out.

And it was the most beautiful sound I'd heard in years.

EIGHTEEN

Laila

"LET 'EM BURN"—NOTHING MORE

Talk about fucking with someone's head. If I wasn't screwed up enough about my identity before, the shit I'd learned was enough to finish the job. The entire time in witness protection, I learned to reinvent myself. The one piece of sanity I held onto was the life I'd had before it had gone to shit.

Now, I didn't even have that.

Though I always knew my parents loved me, I wasn't theirs and they didn't tell me. My mother died before I had a chance to know her. I had a right to know the truth. Instead, I was left feeling it was all a lie.

Lies. Lies. Lies. Lies.

Closing my eyes, I drew in a deep breath and slowly exhaled to get the chant to go away. All that could wait. I'd process it later. The matter at hand was a bit more pressing.

I'd always been a little claustrophobic, and it wasn't helping that I wasn't truly being held in the cell in the dark. The red bulb outside the cell shed very little light in the cold room. The drain in the center of the floor was a dark hole that appeared sinister in the eerie glow.

My gaze lifted to stare at the camera in the top corner of the room that was half cage with the bars across the front. I knew Facet was watching, but it was little consolation.

"Are you still here?" I whispered.

A feathering touch moved down my cheek, and I startled. "I'm here," the emptiness whispered back.

It was easy to forget he was there when I couldn't see a damn thing. Another fortifying breath, and I nodded. The sound of a bullet being chambered made me gasp.

"Just me." The whisper blew over my neck before an invisible kiss pressed to my skin.

Fingers curled tightly around the edge of the wooden bench I sat on, I waited. Finally, footsteps echoed in the stairwell leading to the dank basement. Despite knowing someone was coming, my heart jumped in my throat when the door opened.

Venom was first, and in his gaze was a brief reassurance. Three men in suits followed, with Voodoo and Raptor behind them.

"That's her?" the first man asked. His nose was flat, giving the impression it had been frequently broken. "She looks like a stripper, not a hacker."

My teeth were clenched, and my lip curled.

"I told you we had her. Our man went through her computer, and we have that for you to take to your boss," Venom said.

I glared.

"She looks like she'll be fun to break in," the second one

said, and I wanted to jump up to tell him to fuck off. A soft touch on my back had me biting my tongue and staying seated.

"Open the door. We have a plane to catch. The rest of the money has been transferred as you instructed," Flat-Nose said.

Venom looked to Voodoo and gave him a lift of his chin. Voodoo stepped forward and unlocked the barred door.

"Bind her," Flat-Nose told the third guy, who stepped forward with chains and shackles I hadn't noticed initially. He had yet to say anything.

As he advanced, I shrank back on the bench. Though I knew this wasn't really going to go through, it was truly terrifying thinking anything could go wrong. When he reached for my arm, I panicked and started to jerk away. My foot shot out, and I kicked him.

He shouted in surprise and dropped to his knees. The second man rushed in to assist him in subduing me.

Feeling like a caged animal, I stood on the bench, and my gaze darted back and forth. It didn't matter that Ghost's club told me to play along. It didn't matter that we had a plan. And in their defense, they did ask if I thought I could handle the plan. Living my life constantly being afraid had caught up with me. The second man approached, and I kicked out at him too.

Flat-Nose seemed to curse in a foreign language. "Fuck's sake," he grumbled and stormed in. A fist with brass knuckles drawn back to hit me, he stared at me with cold dark eyes. They sent a chill through me as I braced for the impact, forgetting Ghost and the others were there.

Before he could make contact, he was clutching at his throat with his eyes bulging. A thin indent crossed the column of his neck. After that, everything happened so fast, I lost track of it all.

By the time the metaphorical dust settled, Voodoo and

Raptor had the other two facedown and arms zip-tied behind their backs. The first guy had dropped to the floor like a sack of potatoes, and his lifeless body lay across one of the other guys, who was screaming.

"It's okay," Voodoo said as he held a hand up to me. Trembling, I took it, and he helped me off the bench.

"I've got her," Ghost damn near growled as he immediately appeared next to Voodoo, who smirked at him. He took my hand from Voodoo, and we skirted the men on the floor.

"Aren't you worried that they saw you do that?" I whispered in a shaky voice, casting one last glance back at the dark basement as we climbed the stairs. Though I'd known they would capture the guys who came for me, I didn't expect one to be killed in front of me. My brain was having a hard time processing that it had been Ghost who did it.

"No." His answer was abrupt and unconcerned.

"O-Okay." I chose not to think about why he didn't think it was a big deal.

He helped me in the SUV we'd taken over there and drove from the farm full of pigs back to the clubhouse.

When we went inside, we went to the bar. There wasn't anyone behind it, so Ghost sat me at a stool and went behind to grab a bottle of whiskey. "Want some?" he asked as he held the bottle up.

"No, thank you," I said, knowing if I drank it, I might puke it up.

He grabbed a glass, set it on the bar top, then poured a little in the bottom. He drank it in damn near one swallow, then poured another. It went back as fast. After a third, he set the glass down and dropped his head.

After a moment, he raised his head, and the anguish in his eyes made my chest cave.

"Ghost?" I asked, unable to verbalize my thoughts.

"He was going to hit you. They could've killed you—right in front of my eyes. You were supposed to play along, Laila."

"I know, but you don't understand what was going through my head," I argued.

"I killed a man in front of you!" he shouted.

An older man I'd been introduced to as Hawk, Voodoo's dad, came from the room behind the bar, followed by a prospect carrying a crate of liquor. "What's going on?"

His gaze darted from mine to Ghost's, who wouldn't make eye contact. He placed a hand on Ghost's forearm, and the tension in my man's shoulders immediately eased.

"I fucking hate it when you do that," he said pleasantly, causing Hawk to smirk. Initially, I was confused, then the light bulb went off and I realized the man must have some type of empathic ability. More of those "special abilities" Ghost talked about.

Hawk rested a hand over mine that was twisting a napkin. An instant calm washed through me, and it made me almost sleepy.

Blade came out of the hallway to the members' rooms and cocked a brow.

"Everything okay?" he asked, looking from me to Ghost, to Hawk, to the prospect.

"Just great" was Ghost's chill reply.

"Time for me to go to work?" he asked Ghost.

"Yep."

"Cool. Later," he said and left the building.

"Wanna take a nap?" Ghost asked me with a sleepy smile.

"Sounds perfect," I replied.

He rounded the bar, picked me up, and tossed me over his shoulder.

"Ohhhh, you have a nice ass," I said, since it was right in front of me. Both hands cupped the perfect cheeks encased in denim. "Bet I could bounce quarters off it."

Hawk chuckled, and I looked up through my curtain of pink hair in time to see the prospect duck his head. I happily waved at them as I bounced along over Ghost's broad shoulder.

When we got to the room, we didn't nap.

At least, not right away.

NINETEEN

Ghost

"SOMEBODY TOLD ME"—MOTIONLESS IN WHITE

After a kiss to her brightly colored hair, I left Laila sleeping soundly and naked in my bed. We hadn't been using condoms since reuniting, and I half hoped her birth control would fail. That thought came so quickly and out of the blue that I shocked myself.

Ensuring the door was locked, I gently closed it and made my way out to the common area.

"Feeling better?" Hawk asked me from his spot on the couch in front of the big-screen TV on the wall. A hockey game played, and I watched long enough to know it was the Austin Amurs in the playoffs against Seattle.

"You're an asshole sometimes," I grumbled.

He chuckled, because he knew that his empathic abilities not only calmed me, but also seemed to make me horny as fuck.

Everyone seemed to react differently, but everyone was left with a slightly euphoric feeling.

"You saying you didn't enjoy your 'nap' just now?" He snickered as he raised a beer to his lips.

"Shouldn't you be at home with Julia?" I asked him in a dry tone, not answering his question, because fuck yes, I'd enjoyed myself, but I wanted to be there when they were working on getting information from the Khatri assholes.

"Nope. She's shopping with Kira for clothes that Parker doesn't need but they insist he does." He rolled his eyes.

"Blade still over there?" I asked, knowing he knew what I was asking.

"Yep."

"Cool," I replied, then left to take the path we had that ran from the clubhouse, through the separating field, and to the farm.

I went into the old slaughterhouse that was silent as a tomb, through the rickety-looking door that hid a soundproof one. Slowly descending the stairs, I whistled happily.

As soon as I opened the second soundproof door into the basement, I heard the screams. *Yep, Blade is at work.*

Though I knew better, nothing could've prepared me for what I walked in on.

"What the fuck?" I muttered as I stared. Voodoo, Phoenix, and Squirrel stood off to the side, watching the absolute circus of fuckery take place. None of them seemed to notice the horrid stench.

"I'm actually impressed. And he got confirmation that they have the girl," Squirrel said as he leaned against the wall with his head cocked slightly.

Blade had one of the guys bent over a bench, knees spread, strapped to the legs of the bench. His hairy balls were visible between his legs, and I wrinkled my nose. But that wasn't the twisted part.

The "fucking machine" he'd shown us he'd found online was set up behind the guy, only instead of a silicone dildo like in the video, he had a splintery phallic-shaped piece of wood halfway in the guy's asshole.

"Let me ask you one more time," Blade said as he sat in a chair next to the guy eating a sandwich. "Which island is she on?" He tapped an image that was on the bench in front of the guy's face.

"Fuck you!" the guy said.

"Brave or stupid?" I asked.

"Stupid," Voodoo immediately replied.

"Wrong answer!" Blade said with a sadistic grin. His foot then pressed on what looked like a sewing machine foot peddle, and the "fucking machine" went to work. The dude screamed, making me cringe, and I actually had to look away.

"Fucking hell! That makes my ass hurt looking at it," I said. "How can you watch that?"

Voodoo's head slowly swiveled my direction. His ice blue eyes locked on mine. "This one likes to sodomize the young boys they traffic."

My eyes narrowed, and I turned back to Blade. "Does that have a faster speed?"

Squirrel chortled. "You should see what's going on with the other guy."

I thought he was just hanging from the hooks waiting his turn. When I looked closer, I realized I was wrong. "Oh shit. Damn that looks awful!"

"Wait 'til you see what he's gonna do with it," Phoenix said with a curl of his lips.

I was afraid. The dude had a piece of PVC up his ass with a wire sticking out the bottom.

"Why do these pricks always have to have shit shoved up their asses?" I asked.

"They get what they give," Voodoo said with a shrug. "Especially if it involves children."

"Sick fucks," I said as I grimaced. "Wait, what's in his mouth?"

The guy's mouth was duct taped, and his cheeks were puffed out. He looked a little green.

"You don't wanna know," Squirrel said with a sadistic smirk.

Phoenix scratched his head and gave me a side-eye.

"What did you do?"

"I didn't do anything to him," he said.

"It was the other guy." Voodoo motioned to the guy with the "fucking machine."

"Well, don't keep me in suspense," I prompted.

"Do you see a dick on him?" Squirrel asked.

I blinked once. Then twice. Then once more for good measure.

"Oh holy Mary, mother of God," I said as my face wrinkled in distaste. That explained the smell.

"Couldn't have him bleeding out right away," Phoenix said with a single shoulder shrug. "Blade asked me to cauterize, so I did."

"There is something seriously wrong with you guys. I've seen some shit in my days, but damn. That's just… I don't even have words." I shook my head in disbelief.

"It's not any worse than things we've done in the past. And not much worse than what they did to innocent victims. Whatever gets answers, right?" Voodoo asked as he gave me a half smile.

I filled my cheeks with air, then blew it out. "I guess. But I'm glad Blade handles this part."

There had been times over the years that I did things that could've gotten me thrown in prison for the rest of my fucking life. And though I got that they were the scum of the earth, I'd happily leave the actual torturing to Blade.

Blade looked up, took a bite of his sandwich, and winked at

me. Then he stood up, paused the machine, and walked to the guy hanging from the meat hook.

"Remember what I told you was inside the pipe?" he asked the suspended man as he shoved the last of the sandwich in his mouth. The guy glared until he saw the sadistic grin that lit Blade's face as he reached for the white piece of pipe.

The guy made muffled cries and shook his head.

"I know I'm gonna regret asking, but what's in the pipe?" I quietly asked the boys.

"Barbwire," Phoenix said with a horrified curl of his lip. My eyes widened, and I almost had to laugh at Blade's creativity. He and Squirrel came up with the weirdest shit.

"Get any more answers?" Venom asked as he entered the room. "We don't have a lot of time before their big boss wonders what's taking them so long."

"Maybe soon," Voodoo murmured as he motioned over his shoulder to where Blade was working. Blade ripped the tape off the other guy, and a bloody, spongy blob of what I assumed was the other guy's dick fell to the floor with a splat.

Venom's brow rose, and he gave his head a quick shake. "I've seen and done a lot in my day that didn't faze me, but Christ, I couldn't do shit like that."

"Same," I agreed.

"Let me know if he gets anything useful. No matter what time it is. I'll keep my phone close, but I'm heading home."

The word "home" made me long for what many of my brothers were finding. For years, I'd happily resided in the clubhouse, but each time I had Laila in my arms, I yearned for more. A home with her... and a family.

It seemed crazy, considering I'd been a solid and confirmed lifelong bachelor up until she'd walked back into my life.

"I'm heading out too," I said, the pull to return to Laila an unmistakable need.

"You need us for anything?" Voodoo called out to Blade, who shook his head.

"I'm good," he said.

"I'll stay just in case," Squirrel said, and I chuckled. Like I said, he was a close second to Blade sometimes.

Venom led the way, and the four of us climbed the stairs, securing the doors as we went.

"As soon as we have a location, we'll go in for the girl Laila's been looking for. I just can't risk my brothers and their families by spreading us thin to check all the islands. I know I could likely get some backup from some of the chapters down that way, but I'd prefer to make the extraction as quick as possible, leaving little to no ripples in the mission's wake. Then we follow through with the rest of the plan." Venom sounded weary, and I knew the mantle of president tended to weigh heavy on him at times.

"Sounds good. We might not bring down the entire trafficking ring, but we'll sure as hell cut off a leg to the monster," Voodoo said. We all nodded.

Venom and Voodoo were heading home. They got on their bikes and rode off with a wave. Phoenix and I traipsed across the field to the clubhouse.

"Did I hear Voodoo say his grandmother was coming up for a visit again?" Phoenix asked me as we approached the side door.

"Yeah. She's missing Julia, Parker, and Voodoo," I said with a grin.

"Why doesn't she just move up here?" he asked with a confused frown.

A chuckle escaped me. "She won't leave the swamps—or Yeti." Yeti was Voodoo's grandfather, who was one of the original members of the New Orleans chapter. Though Madame Laveaux never married him and they didn't live together, they had a long-standing love.

We went inside and found the clubhouse empty except for a prospect leaning over the bar watching the TV. He quickly stood upright when he saw us come in.

"Anything I can get you from the bar?" he asked. He was older than the young guys we usually brought in, probably closer to my age, but had been in a support club for years before deciding to move up.

"I'll take a beer," I said, planning to take it with me to the room. "Make that two."

"Shot of Fireball," Phoenix replied. When the prospect set it down, Phoenix touched the edge of the glass, sending flames dancing around the rim before they moved to the surface of the liquor. Then he lifted it to his lips and tossed it back. When he set the glass down, the flames still danced on the rim, and he held out a finger. The flame jumped to his fingertip like a pet. He watched it briefly, then closed the finger in his fist.

I grabbed the necks of both beers in one hand and slapped Phoenix on the shoulder, pulling his attention from his still-clenched fist. He gave me a chin lift and I walked off. When I turned down the hall to my room, I saw Facet with Willow caged between his hands. They were outside his open doorway, and he looked pissed. She darted doe eyes my way before she ducked under his arm and practically sprinted past me.

Brow raised, I gazed at him. "Everything okay?"

He appeared chagrined and ducked his head as he closed his eyes and took a deep breath. Then he looked at me, and the prior chaotic emotions on his face were erased. "Yeah, just trying to keep Willow out of trouble."

"Anything I should know?"

"Nah," he assured me.

Wordless, I stared for a moment, then asked, "You sure?"

"It's all good. Blade get anything yet?"

Nice deflection.

"No, but Voodoo seems to think he will soon."

He nodded, then moved past me to go back in his room.

When I entered the room I was sharing with Laila, I found her sitting at the laptop chatting with someone, her fingers flying over the keyboard. I set one of the beers next to her, and she looked up at me and smiled.

She pulled an earbud out. "Thank you."

"Whatcha workin' on?" I motioned my head toward the dark screen with the old-school-looking black-and-white conversation that told me she wasn't on a typical website.

"It's my client. I was giving him an update and discussing rescue terms. I also contacted Ryan and worked out the plan with him like you wanted. He's contacted the correct agencies, and they are waiting for the word."

"So your client's willing to pay the extraction fee?" I asked, because if he was, I would be leaving soon.

"Once I assured him of your qualifications and terms, he was quite pleased. He's been worried about her," she added with a slight frown.

"You didn't tell him who we were, did you?"

"Do you not know me at all?" she asked with a regal attitude that made me laugh.

"Yeah, I do. So who is this guy?" I pointed at the screen with my bottle.

"Well, part of the dark web is maintaining anonymity," she said with a smirk.

"But?"

"But I know he's a furniture maker in the hills of Tennessee. A friend of a friend gave him a shortcut to the room to ask for help."

I laughed. "Is he dumb?" The dark web was not a place the general public should be playing around with.

"No, just very worried about finding his sister."

"I get it," I conceded.

As I stared at her gorgeous face, I reached out to trail my fingertips over her features. A crease formed between her eyes as she watched me. It dawned on me as I memorized every inch of the woman she'd become that I'd been lonely. It was a feeling I never wanted to experience again. Though I had my brothers and their families, a piece of my soul had been missing. It was her.

"Marry me," I said, and her eyes popped wide.

TWENTY

Laila

"STARDUST"—GEMINI SYNDROME

"What?" I asked, trying to gather the breath he'd stolen with his unexpected question.

He set his bottle on the desk and lowered himself to his knees. Rough hands cradled my face. Steady as a rock, he held my gaze and wet his bottom lip before he said, "That was probably the suckiest of proposals. I told you I loved you, and I told you that you were mine. I don't think just having a house together will be enough for me. I need to know that you're my wife—my other half."

"You know I'm not the same girl you knew all those years ago. I still love you, but I'm not her. Not anymore."

"I know, and I think I love you even more for it. It was your soul I loved before—and that's still there. It's the badass woman you've become that I love now." His expression told me he was feeling like a big fat sap, so I wasn't surprised when he frowned, then gruffly grumbled, "Don't make me throw you over my shoulder again to get you to answer."

I laughed. "Maybe you should spank me instead?"

A wicked grin lifted his lips, and he leaned forward to grip my bottom lip with his teeth. The metal of my lip ring clinked against his teeth before he gently sucked on it and pressed his tongue in to tangle with mine. When he broke free, we were both a little breathless.

His phone vibrated, and he groaned before he pulled it from his pocket. He read the message and sighed. Then he looked up. "I have time for a quickie if you do."

No need to ask me twice, I jumped up out of the chair, completely ignoring the chat I'd been in. My hands went to the hem of his shirt, and his to mine. In frenzied movements, we stripped each other down, and he had me lying on the bed, legs spread, before I could blink.

"God, I wish I had time to worship you properly," he said into my pussy before he swiped his tongue in and up around my clit. Then he demanded, "Over" as he started to flip me to my hands and knees.

"Hurry," I urged, knowing he didn't have much time. His hand cracked against my ass, and my head automatically swiveled to stare at him. Softly, his hand circled and rubbed the now heated area.

"You told me to," he said with a cocked brow. My mouth opened and closed several times, because I didn't know what to say. It seemed wrong to say I kind of liked that.

He wasn't really waiting for a reply, though. The soft tip of his cock probed at my slippery pussy, and I whimpered.

"You want it rough or easy?"

"Fuck me, goddamn it," I ground out as I pushed back in an attempt to get him deeper.

He chuckled. "Greedy."

But he did as I wanted. One hand wound my hair up, and he pulled my head back as the other held my hip in a bruising grip. He slammed home, and it knocked the breath from me with a grunted huff.

"You're mine, Laila," he said as he pounded relentlessly into my eager pussy. The slapping of our bodies with each thrust was a sound I loved almost as much as how good he felt banging the fuck out of me.

"Yours," I agreed—at that point I'd have agreed to damn near anything to ensure he didn't stop.

"This tight, hot cunt is mine, isn't it?" The dirty words were said in a carnal and almost primal growl as he fucked me harder.

"God, yes," I gasped, reveling in how amazing he was in bed.

The hand clenching my hair pulled until I was up on my knees and then he twisted it to turn my head as he captured my mouth in a messy, needy, almost brutal kiss. The other hand moved from my hip up my side to squeeze my breast and pinch my nipple. If the piercings didn't make them sensitive enough, his deft fingers did.

"You feel. So. Mother. Fuckin'. Good." He said each word between a savage thrust. Then his hand skimmed from my breast over my heated flesh to find my oversensitive clit. Mercilessly, he played that little bundle of nerves until he drove me over the edge.

My climax was explosive and damn near violent in its intensity. He stroked twice through my clenching core before he shoved himself so deep, I nearly went numb, and his thick cock pulsed, filling me. Still, he didn't stop, simply slowed as he grunted with each throb of his cock until I could feel our cum running down my inner thighs.

Kisses rained along the side of my neck as we both fought for oxygen. His corded arms wrapped tightly around me and held my sweaty back to his equally slick front.

"Goddamn, baby," he murmured before pressing his lips to the sensitive spot behind my ear.

"That was..." I had no words.

He coughed out a laugh. "I know. But I'm sorry, I have church. Warned you it would be quick."

"Mmm, okay," I said, ready to curl up in the sheets that smelled like his perfect blend of sexy man.

We both let out a disappointed groan when he slipped free. Our combined release painted my thighs worse than before, but I honestly didn't give two shits.

"Wait here," he murmured, then got off the bed.

Unable to keep myself upright, I dropped face-first into his pillow.

A chuckle echoed in the bathroom as water ran in the sink.

He was so silent on his return, chills hit me when he kissed the divots above my ass. He trailed kisses up and down my spine before he washed me with a warm cloth. When he finished, I languidly stretched and rolled over.

Appreciatively, I watched his muscles ripple under his tanned skin as he dressed.

Jesus, the man was an Adonis.

Once he'd covered all that delectable flesh, he pulled his hair back and secured it, watching me the entire time. His gaze was heated despite the bone-melting fucking he'd already given me.

"I'll be back as soon as I can. Maybe you could look for houses online while I'm gone, yeah?"

"Mmmm, okay," I said with a satisfied tip of my lips. "And the answer to your earlier question is yes."

His grin was almost blinding in its beauty as he approached the bed. Resting his hands next to me, he leaned down to give me one last kiss before he left the room.

Holy shit. After eleven years, I was finally going to be Mrs. Lucian Stone.

Clicking away on my mouse to look at picture after picture, I was deep in the house hunt when my door opened again.

"I've found several possibilities, but I'm not sure exactly where you want to be or how big," I said, but stopped talking when I saw his expression.

"I have to go," he said.

"Go where?" I asked, suddenly worried and on the edge of panicking.

"I'm not able to say exactly at this time, but we think we found the woman you're looking for."

I jumped up from my seat. "You found the island? You need to take me with you."

"Hell, no. We already discussed this. It's going to be dangerous as fuck, and I don't want you anywhere near it. Do you remember what you're supposed to do?" We had come up with a plan as soon as they had Khatri's men. Since we had no idea how long it would be before we had something to go on, they wanted to be prepared for action. I hadn't said anything at the time about going because I was afraid they'd tell me no, and I was right.

"Yes. As soon as I get the call that you have the target secured, I call Ryan, who notifies his friends with the FBI that are on standby with the Coast Guard." I rattled it all off like I was a flight attendant going over preflight checks.

Though I wanted to argue about going with, I knew I wouldn't get him to budge. Unhappily resigned, I sighed. "Do you know how long you'll be?"

He shook his head.

"When do you leave?" I asked, hoping I'd be able to have a few moments with him.

"Now."

"Jesus. Okay." It really wasn't. I was freaking the fuck out inside, but I knew he didn't need to be worrying about me.

"Keep your phone on you for our call. You know what to do," he said, and I nodded.

We moved at the same time, and my arms flew around him as he wrapped me in a tight embrace. "I fucking love you," he said, causing me to smile.

"I love you too. Please be careful," I said into the soft fabric of his chambray shirt.

"Always."

Reluctantly, we parted. He sifted his fingers through my hair as his pale gaze drank me in.

"Can you give me some search criteria before you go? Buy, rent, size, location?" I asked, trying to lighten the somber mood.

"Close to the clubhouse, if you can find something. Other than that, whatever you like. If you want to buy, we buy. If you're not ready to decide, we rent."

I nodded.

He gave me one last passionate kiss, and there was a knock on the door. "Yeah?" he called, barely pulling away from my mouth.

"It's go time!" whoever was waiting said.

"I'll see you soon," he said firmly before he was gone.

I dropped back into the chair and wrapped my arms around myself, already wishing they were his. We'd been apart for years and handled it; why it was suddenly crushing was a mystery. Then I prayed he'd be home soon and safe. I also prayed they found the young woman unharmed, but in the back of my mind, I prepared for the worst.

TWENTY-ONE

Ghost

"WWYDF"—ZERO 9:36

I hated leaving Laila behind, but we needed to deal with this for several reasons. Besides rescuing the woman Laila had found, we had been trying to shut down this trafficking ring for what seemed like forever. The fact that they had used us in the past and we unknowingly helped the very people we were trying to stop really pissed us off.

Then there was the fact that Rudra Khatri was a sick fuck. As we suspected after we found they hired someone besides us, they were into much more than porn and high-end prostitution. Once he'd learned the breach was a woman, he had planned to do some really demented things to Laila. Besides that, he was a lead man in the trafficking ring. Which was why we needed to take him out, then we'd hunt down his brothers. We had the intel from one of the guys Blade worked over that said Rudra would be on the is-land because that was where they were supposed to deliver Laila.

There was the possibility that someone else would pick up the reins, but we would ensure there was enough damage to their operation that they would struggle to get that leg of it up and run-ning again, if at all.

We'd arrived in Jacksonville on a late afternoon flight. A pros-pect and Winchester, the chapter's SAA, had picked us up, and we dropped our shit off at the clubhouse. We went over the plan with their pres, Creed; their VP, Reaper; Winchester; and their enforcer, Justice. Once we had everything set, we headed out and were waiting for one of their prospects to show up with the boat.

It was dark as we waited in the blackest of shadows over by the trees at the edge of the sand. Dressed in black tactical gear from head to toe, we easily blended in. A soft evening breeze blew, but the peaceful serenity of the night was deceiving. It was almost enough to fool someone into thinking there weren't nefarious ac-tivities underway.

"There he is," Justice said as a boat approached. We cautiously left the darkest shadows and crossed to the dock. One by one, we slipped on the deck and dispersed to seats.

"Damn. This is one helluva nice boat. How much did it run you?" I asked, impressed.

Winchester grinned. "Someone owed us money."

Justice snorted a laugh, and we headed out to sea.

"We'll travel across the water in blackout and cut the main engines when we get close," Winchester said.

"Angel, you'll remain on the boat when we go in," Hawk clari-fied. As the senior member, he was in charge of this mission. Angel nodded, knowing that his safety was imperative in case there were injuries during the extraction.

We went over every detail of the plan one last time with the

Jacksonville brothers as we crossed the dark water. Wind whipped at our dark clothing, and sea spray hit us on particularly rough patches.

Finally, we could see distant lights. Justice pointed. "Like I told you at the clubhouse, we'll go in on the south side of the island. That side doesn't actually have access. Our surveillance that Fingers pulled shows the idiots leave it mostly unguarded. It's rocky, but there is a spot we can get close enough for us to take the rubber raiding craft in. Then we climb."

We went covert as Winchester had said we would and moved in. We all checked our weapons one last time and screwed suppressors on them. When we were as close as we could get, we dropped anchor and lowered the inflatable raiding craft into the water.

"You have one hour—no more. That's how often they switch out the guard on the south side. Once that happens, the jig is up and all hell might break loose. You need to be back here with the girl before that time." Justice gave me a somber stare. He knew as well as I did that it wouldn't be easy.

"Got it," Hawk said, then we climbed from the deck to the smaller boat. Those going ashore were me, Hawk, Phoenix, and Winchester.

It wasn't long before we were trolling through the rocky coastline. When we literally bumped up against what appeared to be a thirty-foot cliff, I took a fortifying breath.

This is gonna be fun.

"Jesus, it didn't look that tall in the pictures," Phoenix muttered quietly.

Winchester whispered, "You scared?"

"Everyone shut up. It's doable. Let's move," Hawk softly said, leaving no room for argument. Winchester would stay with the boat and keep watch from there; it would only be the three of us who went in.

Weapon slung over my back, I'd already hooked my gloved hands on the rocks and begun to climb. At least it wasn't as straight up as it looked. By the time I crested the top, my brothers were hot on my heels. There was no sign of the supposed guard as I pulled my body onto the ground.

Using hand signals, we spread out to check the patrol area that Fingers had marked on the aerial view of the island.

Other than the wind blowing through the palm trees, there wasn't a sound. Confused, I looked to Hawk for guidance. That's when I caught the movement. Dude had his back to us and was pissing in the shadows. Ensuring Winchester was still down with the boat, Phoenix looked to me and gave me a nod.

Because I knew the Jacksonville brothers were watching through a range finder, I moved into the shadows and vanished. Like the ghost I was, I closed in on the guy shaking his dick off and putting it back in his pants.

Before he knew what was happening, he had a pistol upside the head and I had his comms. Hawk and Phoenix joined me, and I went visible again. After securing the asshole's hands and feet, then gagging him, I used the device Facet sent with us. Hawk opened the guy's eye, and I did a retinal scan and waited for the results from Facet.

When it came back that he was a registered sex offender of children under the age of twelve, Hawk's eyes went dull, and he snapped the guy's neck. We quickly dragged him off into the trees and grabbed palm fronds to toss over him. We removed his restraints, and if we were able, he'd go over the edge on our way out.

In a few short minutes, the house was in view. Disgusting in its opulence, bright lights shining from the floor-to-ceiling windows and doors made it appear to glow in the dark night.

Our problem was we had no idea exactly where the girl was being held, and it was a huge house. There were several guards on the balconies that came off the floor-to-ceiling glass doors that were slid open to enjoy the ocean breeze, but they didn't seem concerned with safety. After all, they were on a private island miles off the coast of Florida, and they believed they could see the only way to enter the island.

Hawk motioned for me to disappear, so I did and made my way around the house to decide the best way in undetected. The walk-out under the guards was locked up tight as a drum. Curtains were pulled, making it impossible to see inside.

In the end, I walked up the stairs and right past the guards, then through the open glass doors behind them. Silent as a wraith, I went room by room. Periodically, I placed the cameras that Facet had handed me before we left. As loud as they were playing the music, I could've stomped through, but I wasn't taking the chance. The main living area was pretty open, and all I saw were a few men I recognized as a Fortune 500 CEO, a senator from California, and a movie star, all snorting coke off the kitchen island.

Bypassing them, I moved down the hall. As cautiously as I could, I opened the doors a crack as I passed down the hall. One had a white ass in the air passed out with a woman who was sleeping too. Her hair and skin were dark and didn't match the subject's description. I hated that we didn't have the manpower to just take out all the assholes involved in this cesspool. Sticking to the plan, I kept going. The quicker I found the woman we were looking for, the quicker we could get the rest of the women out of there.

Some of the things I saw in the other rooms made me anxious to get our girl and get out so we could make the call ASAP.

If I thought we could get away with it, I would've dragged the women out and had Phoenix burn the island into the ocean. There were too many people there though. We'd never pull it off. We were good, but we were severely outnumbered.

Careful of the stairs and possible creaking, I descended to

the lower level. The first door I opened had two women sitting on a chaise lounge, bound and gagged, but made up like they were going out on the town. One saw the movement of the door and her eyes went wide, but when it didn't go further, she appeared to relax slightly. The other looked vacant and didn't move.

Stick to the plan. Stick to the plan.

The next door made my mouth fall open before I grinned evilly. The man making a woman dance for him who looked high as hell was none other than former senator Damon. The sick fuck was sitting on a couch stroking his dick as he petted another woman who was kneeling next to him—like she was a goddamn dog.

Motherfucker. We got you.

Though I wanted to put a bullet between his eyes, I had a job to do. He'd get his soon.

When I was about to call it a loss because I hadn't come across the woman we were looking for, I noticed five small doors in the last empty room. They were the width of an average door, but each one was only about three feet tall with a peephole toward the top. There was a dark wood cabinet next to them, a four-poster bed, and dresser. *What the fuck?*

I tried the first door, prepared for anything. It was locked. Glancing through the peephole, all I saw was black. What the actual fuck could be behind the small doors that needed keys to get in but had peepholes?

Letting my rifle hang at my front from the sling, I pulled out the small lock pick set and worked the keyhole until I was able to get the lock to release.

When I cautiously opened the door a crack, movement made me close it again. I had no idea what the holy hell was in there. That was when I noticed there was two small switches at the top of each door.

Unsure of my next move, I glanced around. Time was ticking,

but I didn't hear anyone out in the hall yet. Taking a chance that whatever was in there couldn't see me, I flipped the first switch as I looked through the peephole.

"No fucking way," I whispered as I watched a naked woman scurry to the back of the tiny room, crouch in the corner, and stare in fear through tangled strands of hair at the door. She didn't look like the subject, but it was hard to tell with her hair hanging in her face.

Unsure, I risked using my comm and tugged the sheet off the bed. "We have an issue."

"What the fuck?" Hawk replied so softly, I almost didn't hear him.

"No sign of the subject, yet, but I think there's women in small cage-like rooms down here. She could be in one, and I can't leave the rest in there."

I thought I heard whispered curses. "We're running out of time, and you know we have limited space and manpower. Just use your judgement unless you can get us in."

There was a window, but I had no idea if it had alarms activated.

"Negative."

"Do what you have to do."

Again, I cracked the door and whispered inside, "We're here to help. Are you able to come out?"

"Who are you?" a heavily accented voice asked with a noticeable tremor to it.

"Friends. Come out slowly," I told her. Fuck, I really didn't want to hurt her, but if she screamed or tried to attack me or run, I was prepared. Deciding I better not make myself appear in front of her, I did it before I opened the door further.

She slowly crawled toward the door. I handed her the sheet as I fully opened the door, and her gaze darted around in confusion.

The terror in her haunted eyes was unmistakable as she snatched the sheet.

"Do you know if there are other women in there?" I motioned to the other doors.

She nodded with a furrowed brow as she wrapped the sheet around herself.

"What's your name?" I asked her as I prepared to pick the next lock.

"Maria."

"Do you know the other women?"

She shrugged and nodded but seemed uncertain.

"Inessa speaks no English," she said, pointing at the next door.

"Can you translate? Tell her we're getting you out and not to scream?"

She nodded, then crouch walked to the next door. That's when I noticed she had a fucking dog collar on and her back was covered in angry red welts—some raw and open. I felt ill.

She frantically whispered through the next door. When I went to pick the lock, she cocked her head. Then she pointed at the wooden cabinet. I picked the lock and opened the doors to find five keys hanging on the inside of one door, and the rest of the cabinet filled with vicious-looking items. It was beyond BDSM. They were things designed to seriously harm someone.

When she pointed at the second key, I handed it to her, then took the third key to the third door. A dark-haired woman came out of that second door and clung to Maria. I avoided staring at their nudity.

I tossed Maria the fourth key and grabbed the fifth as I stuck mine in the lock of the third and asked, "Are there clothes in here anywhere?"

Maria went to the closet and pulled out several short silk

robes. Inside, I cursed, but they were better than nothing. "Use the right switch," Maria said, and I nodded.

The woman sat in the corner rocking with her back to the door and her arms wrapped tightly around her legs. "I'm turning the light on. Can you come out? I'm here to help," I repeated to her as I'd told Maria. Instead of the bright blinding light I'd shone on Maria, it was an amber-colored one.

Slowly her head turned. Her wheat-colored hair was tucked behind her ear, and she peeked over her shoulder at me. Gray-blue eyes damn near stared through my soul, but she didn't make a move to come out.

"Eliska?" I asked and watched her eyes widen in surprise. Then she nodded.

"I'm here to take you home," I said, and a tear ran down her cheek. "We need to hurry."

Pressing one arm over her breasts, she crawled out on one arm and her knees, then curled in a protective position. I held my hand out to Maria for a robe. When she gave it to me, I draped it over Eliska's shoulders, and she carefully put her arms through the sleeves. Not before I saw the bite marks on her, though.

"Jesus," I whispered and immediately regretted that it slipped out because silent tears coursed down her cheeks.

"What about the last door?" I asked the women.

"There are only four of us right now. The fifth... she... she's gone, and they haven't replaced her," Maria whispered.

I didn't want to think about what that meant, because regardless, we were too late for her.

Looking into four sets of frightened eyes, I was torn. I was only supposed to bring Eliska. The rest would be rescued by the FBI when they came in. But what if something happened and they didn't make it in time? Or the assholes running the house killed them when they got raided?

I couldn't leave them.

Roughly, I rubbed my gloved hand over my mouth.

"Do you think you can keep up?" I asked them. They nodded. Barefoot, naked except for a flimsy, short robe, they were so desperate for freedom they were willing to leave like they were.

I pulled out the pistol strapped to my thigh, and Inessa gasped. "Shhhh," I said, placing a finger over my lips. When Maria comforted her, I checked my weapon again.

"If I have to use this, please do *not* scream. I'm trying to get you out of here with the least amount of disruption. The people here outnumber us by a long shot." They all nodded at my request. I motioned them to follow me.

"Is there a way out on this level that won't set off an alarm?" I asked.

Maria appeared worried. "No."

"Shit. Okay, we're going out the way I came in," I muttered. Except I would be completely visible to anyone we came across.

Hawk was going to fucking kill me—if we made it out alive.

"Stay close," I told them, praying they'd listen as we started up the stairs.

Maria clutched my shirt as I began to turn toward the living area I'd entered. Brow furrowed in question, I glanced over my shoulder at her.

She pointed in the opposite direction. When I looked that way, I remembered nothing but bedrooms. When I shook my head, she angrily pointed to the door at the end of the hall.

"Down there!" she forcefully whispered.

I had no clue why I believed her, but she seemed adamant, and I knew there were likely three or more people in the living area.

We rushed as silently as we could to what I hoped was an exit.

She pointed at the door again to ensure I knew we were at

the right one. We walked into what had to be a master bedroom but had been turned into a kinky one.

Anxiety hit me when there were no exterior doors. But before I could lose my shit, Maria grabbed my arm and dragged me toward what I guessed was a closet or the bathroom.

As I reached for the knob, the door opened and a dude looking straight out of an eighties porn was staring at me. He immediately scrambled for a pistol sitting on the marble bathroom counter, but I was quicker.

A bullet between his dark eyes, and we were stepping over his crumpled form.

Maria spit on him as we did, and the rest of the girls did the same.

Not that I held guilt for what I'd done, but I was relieved to know I'd been able to give them some sort of vengeance.

The bathroom was damn near as big as the bedroom, and on one wall, there were floor-to-ceiling windows with French doors in the center.

"Nice," I murmured as I unlocked the handle and we hurried out onto the deck. Maria gave me a smug grin, which caused me to shake my head.

There was a set of stairs that led down to the beach at the side of the house. We hurried down, and I reached out to Hawk on the comms.

"Coming around from the side stairs," I said.

"Copy that," Hawk replied.

How I made it safely out of the house with four half-dressed women was a miracle. There was no explanation other than that. In our wake was only one guy with a bullet between his eyes, and I counted that a success.

The look on Hawk's face as we came around the corner of the house would've been comical in any other situation.

"This was not the plan," he softly growled.

"We don't have time. We need to move," I said, and he gave me a narrow-eyed stare. He was right because it was a matter of short time before what we'd done was discovered.

Phoenix, Hawk, and I hustled the four women across the plush lawn and through the bordering brush. I was worried about their bare feet, but not a one of them complained as we hurried as fast as we could with them.

We reached the drop-off knowing we had mere minutes to spare. Hawk called Winchester on the comms and explained the situation. Winchester cursed but agreed.

"We're going to have to lower one down, then the other three will go down with us," Hawk said, and four sets of eyes widened.

"Lower me first," Maria said as she stepped forward.

Hawk nodded, and we fastened the harness around her as Phoenix gave her a quiet crash course in rappelling. We tied the rope off to a palm tree. Her feet were likely going to be torn the fuck up by the time she got to the boat, but I hoped it wouldn't be too bad.

It seemed to take forever. Finally, Winchester was helping her into the boat and out of the harness so we could retrieve it.

"What about that guy?" I asked, motioning over my shoulder toward where the guard was in the trees.

"Leave him." Hawk shook his head, and I swallowed hard. I still didn't regret taking the women with me. In fact, I wished I could've grabbed them all.

Next, Phoenix went down with Inessa strapped tightly to him.

Once they were safely in and I had the harness secured, I went down with Eliska. Halfway down, the rope seemed to slip, and we dropped quickly until I was able to get a grip. Eliska let out a squeak, but to her credit, she didn't scream. Even through the gloves, my hands burned.

We were settling into the boat as Hawk came down with the last woman. I still didn't know her name because we hadn't had time for further introductions.

"It's going to be slow going because we're overloaded," Winchester said.

The women appeared frightened.

"We'll be okay; we just can't rush," he gruffly explained.

It seemed to take hours to make the trip back to the boat. Once we were alongside it, they helped us all aboard.

Winchester had obviously notified them we had extra guests, because no one seemed surprised.

As soon as everyone was on the boat, we pulled the inflatable craft up and deflated it. The anchor was next as I helped get us underway. Then we were on the move. By then we were slightly out of breath from adrenaline and rushing to get our asses out of there.

"Take the women below and get them something to drink," Winchester told Justice. "Angel, you're the one with medic experience. You may want to join them."

"On it," Angel gruffly agreed as he and Hawk went down into the cabin.

I made the call to Laila as soon as we were far enough out. I wanted to talk to her longer, but I needed to stay focused. We weren't in the clear yet.

After the women were out of the picture and Justice came back up, every weapon was wiped, disassembled, and placed in two weighted, waterproof trunks. When we were probably halfway between the island and Jacksonville, we slowed down. Phoenix and I looked at Winchester like they were nuts. Then the boxes went over the side and quickly sank in the dark waves.

"Are you sure that's a good idea?" Phoenix asked Winchester.

The SAA for the Jacksonville chapter chuckled as he flashed

a white smile. "We know where to find them if and when we need them. If they get found, there's nothing to tie them to us."

I left that one alone. Whatever worked for them.

The rest of the ride was silent except for the sound of the motor and the splash of the water we sped through. The women were still in the cabin being checked over by Angel and Hawk. It made me sick to think of what they might've endured. I glanced at the stairs that led to the cabin.

"Don't worry, my brother," Justice said as his hair blew wildly, obscuring his dark eyes momentarily. "We'll go back and take care of them if the plan falls through. We'll also ensure the other three women are safe and taken care of. You have papers for yours?"

"Yes," I replied. Eliska was the sister of Laila's client, and we had IDs generated for her since we had no idea where her purse and belongings had gone. We were meeting her brother at a bar near the Nashville airport.

The lights on the shore of Jacksonville drew closer, and I breathed a sigh of relief. We headed back to the dark cove where we started.

Footsteps on the stairs grabbed my attention, and I glanced over my shoulder to see Angel coming up, followed by Hawk. Neither looked happy.

"Ghost, a word," Angel said, and moved to the bow of the boat.

"Excuse me, brother. I'll be right back," I told Winchester. He nodded, and I followed Angel, who stood with his legs braced and a hand over his mouth as he stared out into the dark cove.

"What's the problem?" I asked.

"Eliska says she doesn't have a brother."

TWENTY-TWO

Laila

"BULLETPROOF"—FROM ASHES TO NEW

Unable to sleep, I was messing around on my computer. My phone rang, and I snagged it as I swiped the screen in one motion. "Ghost?"

"Make the call," he said, sounding out of breath. "Hurry."

"Are you okay?"

"Call!" he said, and the line went dead.

Panic hit me, but I dialed Ryan's number on the phone Facet had given me.

"Ryan," I blurted out as soon as he picked up.

"Goddamn it, Laila. What the hell took so long?" he asked without preamble. We had spoken after I talked to my client, and he had contacted me that night to tell me he had shit in order. When I asked him who would be there and if he could guarantee they would be able to raid the island after the guys extracted my client's sister, he told me he couldn't divulge that but to rest assured they were going to swarm the island on my okay. They agreed to let us extract Eliska first, which shocked me. It made me wonder what the hell kind of pull Ryan had.

"Not now, Ryan. Listen and prepare to copy," I said in a rush.

"Speak," he said, suddenly all business.

I rattled off the confirmed coordinates to the island Ghost had given me. "All clear."

I heard clicking noises that sounded like he was typing.

"They're going in. But remember, Laila, we're going to talk. Soon," he said, and he ended the call. I tried to call Ghost back, but it went straight to voicemail.

I curled up on the bed and wrapped my arms around his pillow. Pressing my face into the case, I breathed in his scent, trying to calm myself.

Please let him be okay.

The sound of shouting woke me, and I sat up. Initially disoriented, I was surprised I'd actually fallen asleep. Pounding feet followed. Curiosity had me out of bed and shoving my feet in a pair of flip-flops. Were the guys back so soon?

When I peeked out the door, Squirrel was running past barefoot and pulling on a shirt. That had me more confused than ever.

Cautiously, I followed Squirrel. I'd barely turned the corner where I had a view of the common area when three shots fired. Sabre stumbled and fell as his gun clattered on the ground. He was followed by E, who dropped to his knees holding his upper chest.

Heart slamming against my ribs, I froze.

"Put the weapons down, or we'll mow you all down and not bat an eye," a cold voice said.

From where I stood, I could see one man with a gun trained on Raptor, Facet, a prospect, and Kicker, but I couldn't see anyone else. Nor could I see who was talking. Slowly, they placed their weapons on the ground, but I could tell they weren't happy about it.

A hand covered my mouth, and I screamed into it. Nothing but a muffled squeak came out, but it was enough that the man with a gun heard.

"Shit!" the man behind me cursed as the gunman turned his weapon on us.

A man in khakis and a short-sleeved shirt stepped further into the room to see what the other man was focused on. When he looked at us, I would've sworn I was looking straight into the eyes of the devil himself. Nausea churned my guts.

"Well, look who we have here. The prodigal son and my long-lost daughter. Two birds—one stone," the man said, and my stomach dropped.

That was when I knew I was looking at my biological father—Luis Trujillo.

My spine stiffened. *What did he mean by prodigal son?*

"Well, come out and join the party!" Luis said with a smile, as if we were truly attending a gala instead of two men bleeding out on the ground as we were held at gunpoint.

Unable to move, I stood fast until Blade stepped up next to me and curled a hand around my arm to lead me forward. "I've got you," he whispered, and I didn't even see his lips move.

With leaden feet, I moved out into the common area. Blade kept step with me, and true to his word, he never let go. When we stood next to Raptor, we stopped, and I swallowed hard. There were nine men holding automatic rifles on Ghost's brothers that were remaining.

"Can't say I approve of the tattoos and all that metal in your face, but I can see your mother in you. God rest her soul," he said with mock solemnity.

"How dare you speak of her!" I might not have known she was my mother, and I might not remember her, but she gave birth to me. I wasn't about to have this low-life piece of shit mock her death. I moved forward to lash out at him, but Blade held me back.

"What do you want?" Blade demanded.

"What do I want? Why, I want what any dad wants... to get to know my daughter." The evil grin that split his face sent a foreboding chill down my spine. The fact that he called himself my "dad" made me want to vomit.

"No." Blade stared at him with a colder than usual glint to his eyes. I'd had minimal interactions with him. The man could be scary as fuck. Right now, I was glad he was on my side.

"No?"

"You heard me."

"I don't believe I asked you. However, you have a debt yet to be paid to me. Did you think I forgot?" Luis said to Blade with a smirk.

His smile fell, and he motioned to his men. "Secure them."

I could sense the rage emanating off Raptor, Blade, and the others. Three of the nine men went around and zip-tied the RBMC members and lined them up on the floor against the wall. The others continued to train their automatic rifles on them.

Me and Blade, they left standing.

That's when I realized Squirrel was missing. Yet I knew I'd seen him run past my room.

"Get them. Let's go. I can't stand being near that pig farm in this godforsaken state any longer," Luis instructed his men.

"We need to stall," I heard Blade whisper.

"Wait! Please," I blurted. It had the desired effect, because Luis paused and looked slowly over his shoulder.

He cocked a brow and waited for me to continue. For the life of me, I couldn't see a thing we had in common other than the color of our hair. While mine had been very fair as a child and young adult, it had darkened with age to a light brown. It was how I'd gotten away with dyeing the top by my roots dark and the bottom pink. As it grew out, it wasn't super noticeable.

"I um, I need my purse and my papers," I stammered.

"My dear girl, don't fuck with me. Your papers are all fake, so you won't need them. Besides, I'll have new ones made for you anyway."

"Fine," I huffed. "But why do you even want anything to do with me? I'm nearly thirty years old. You've had nothing to do with my whole life, but I'm supposed to believe you want to get to know me now?"

"First of all, I don't owe you any explanations, but I'm feeling generous considering the circumstances. I'm sure you already know that your family hid your existence from me. It was actually quite brilliant that your uncle and his wife pretended you were theirs. Had I known you were mine when I had them killed, I would've had my men take you instead of shooting you—not that you were supposed to be shot, but I digress. Faking your death and witness protection was also quite smart. Until my well-paid man overheard one of those idiots with the US Marshals discussing your case, I actually believed it. Except you made one foolish mistake." He was so smug and condescending, I wanted to slap him.

"What's that?" I asked.

"You hacked into my partner's business."

My eyes closed. Of all the stupid and ridiculous coincidences.

"Now that I've found you again, you perfectly wrapped up a problem I've been dealing with."

"How?" Not that I cared, but I was doing my best to keep him talking like Blade had said.

"Lila." He sighed my old name. "Enough fucking around, unless you'd like me to kill your new friends. I'm on a schedule."

One of the men pushed me and Blade from behind, and I stumbled. Blade growled deep in his chest and caught me before I fell. Then he shot a vicious glare at the man who had pushed me.

They took us out to a waiting SUV. There was another SUV that was mangled as bad as the tall fence it had plowed through. Two men climbed in the far back, two men up front, and me sandwiched between Luis and Blade.

"I honestly wasn't expecting the extra passenger. I'm impressed that you hid so well, Finley. Who would've thought I'd find you both in the same place? Must be my lucky day."

Blade's name is Finley?

"Fuck you," Blade said through clenched teeth.

Luis simply chuckled before he stared at me, then shook his head. "I hope your new husband won't be angry at all that shit you've done to your skin."

"Husband?" I asked in absolute shock as we started to pull out of the lot.

Before Luis could elaborate, I heard a weird gasping sound from the back seat. Then there was blood spraying all over me. I couldn't help it, I screamed. Motion in the back seat caught my attention, and I thought I saw Squirrel crouched on the men back there, but I blinked and he was gone.

Blade jumped forward, snapped the passenger's neck, and had the dead man's gun held to the driver's head faster than anything I'd ever seen.

"Stop the car," he told the driver, who pulled off to the shoulder and cast a worried glance in the rearview mirror. Evidently what he saw shocked the hell out of him, because his complexion went white before his door was jerked open.

Squirrel was standing there with a twisted grin. "Hi," he said to the guy with a happy little wave of his bloody hand.

I started to hyperventilate.

"Laila!" Blade called. "Hold it together for me. We're okay. It's over."

Terrified, I was still taking gasping breaths as I nervously glanced to my left. Luis was sitting there with blank eyes and his throat gaping like a macabre smile. Blood was *everywhere*.

For a second, I was transported back to the night my parents died, and I couldn't shake it. It was all the blood.

Blade gripped my face and forced me to look at him. In my periphery, I saw Squirrel shove the driver, who was now obviously dead, over into the passenger seat on top of the other dead guy and climb in.

"Look at me," Blade demanded. "It's okay."

Squirrel made a U-turn on the highway and headed back past the clubhouse. We pulled into the hog farm Ghost had told me they owned. The entire time, I stared into Blade's eyes, trying not to completely lose my shit.

"I'm gonna be sick," I whimpered.

Blade quickly turned my head, and I puked all over Luis's lap. The sight of my vomit on top of all the blood was more than I could handle, and I began to laugh. The more I laughed, the more maniacal and disconnected it sounded to my ears.

Squirrel opened the door, and Blade helped me out of his side.

"Get her inside and washed up. You'll have to put a sheet around her until we can get her back to the clubhouse," I heard. In a daze, I turned and looked at Venom's salt-and-pepper beard, then up to his stern expression.

"She's going into shock," I heard and then saw Voodoo standing there next to Venom as everything began to blur. Blade held me up when my knees buckled.

Venom stepped in front of me and laid a hand on my cheek. As he spoke, I began to relax. "Laila," he said. "It's over. We're going to take care of everything, but I need you to get cleaned up. Do you think you can do that?"

Numbly, I nodded. A woman took my hand, and I slowly swiveled my head to look into Loralei's worried gaze.

"I'll help you get cleaned up," she said kindly. Slowly, I glanced down where our hands connected and saw the contrast of my blood-splattered one against her clean one. Blankly, I stared a moment before I looked up and nodded.

She led me into a metal building that looked like a slaughterhouse. We went around a wall and into a walk-in shower.

"Can you undress? Or do you need my help?" she asked.

I blinked once, then my gaze darted over to the stainless steel walls and floor with a drain.

"I can do it," I mumbled.

Her brow furrowed, but she nodded. "Okay, I'll stand around the corner, but I'll be right here if you need me. You hand your clothes around to me, and I'll give you some soap. Okay?"

"Okay," I whispered.

"When you're done, the towel is right here," she said as she motioned to a hook she was hanging it on.

As soon as she stepped around the wall like she'd promised, I stripped out of the clothes that were already starting to stiffen from the thick blood drying on them.

I held my arm out with the clothes, and she held open a black trash bag that I dropped them in. Somehow, I knew I'd never see those clothes again, but I sure as hell didn't care.

As I washed, the water ran rusty-colored, and I tried not to think about the blood being from my biological father. A man who was a criminal of the worst sort who had killed my parents and likely my aunt—shit, mother. And I was a part of him. What did that say about me? To say I was stunned and shaken was an understatement.

"You doing okay?" Loralei called, and it made me jump as it echoed off the stainless steel walls.

"Yes," I said, giving myself a final rinse before I shut off the water and grabbed the towel. Using more force than was necessary, I dried my skin until it was bright pink in the areas I wasn't tattooed.

"Blade brought this in for you," she said as she held out a T-shirt I recognized as one of Ghost's. I quickly pulled it over my head and removed the towel from underneath. It was damn near a dress on me, but it was comforting knowing it was Ghost's.

She set a pair of flip-flops down for me to step into. "Blade ran back to the clubhouse and grabbed the first thing he saw. I have no idea why he didn't grab you your own clothes. He's a man, though."

"Thank you," I murmured and put one foot at a time into the shoes. I had no idea who they belonged to, and I didn't care.

For a second, she appeared conflicted. "Laila, I know this is a lot. Tonight had to have been terrifying for you. Ghost may come across as gruff or a prankster at times, but he has a good heart. What none of us realized was that it belonged to you. There are a lot of things about this family that may seem, uh, unconventional, but I promise you, they will always have your back."

Blinking rapidly, I frowned and cocked my head in question.

"I just hope this didn't scare you away," she clarified, and understanding dawned.

I inhaled deeply before letting it out. "No. This hasn't scared me away. I've seen a lot of shit. It's just the shock of everything, not to mention coming face-to-face with the man who not only killed my parents, but sired me was a little overwhelming." I refused to refer to that evil person as my father ever again.

"Okay, good." She breathed a sigh of relief. "Venom wants

me to give you a ride back to the clubhouse while they take care of… things."

"Thank you," I said to her. For the first time in years, I actually felt like I had a friend and a family. "Has anyone heard from Ghost?" I asked.

Her expression told me the answer before she sadly shook her head.

Tears tracked my cheeks as we drove back to the clubhouse. I prayed Ghost would come back to me soon.

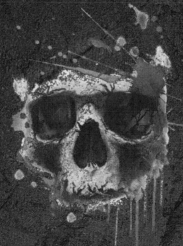

TWENTY-THREE

Ghost

"KEEP THE DOGS AT BAY"—SEETHER

The sky was barely starting to lighten when we reached the Jacksonville clubhouse. Bone weary, I wanted a hot shower, a bed, and to call Laila. Not necessarily in that order.

A soon as I was shown to the room I'd be sharing with Phoenix, I pulled out my phone. Three times I called Laila, but it kept going to voicemail.

"What the fuck?" I asked, staring at my phone like it was a foreign object.

Phoenix walked in, kicking his boots off. I glanced up, and he looked as ass-dragging as I was.

"Hawk said you need to call Venom."

My guts tightened. "Did he say why?"

"No, he called to give him the rundown, and as soon as he ended the call, he told me to tell you to contact Venom ASAP, so here I am." He shrugged, then fell back on the bed. "No spooning tonight. I'm tired, and you'll make me sweat."

"Dick," I said with a half-hearted chuckle as I was already calling Venom.

"Ghost," Venom said when he answered.

"Yeah, what's up, boss man?" As soon as I finished with whatever he wanted, I would ask if Laila was still sleeping.

"Before you lose your shit, she's okay."

"Saying something like that is guaranteed to make me lose my shit," I practically growled. "What the fuck happened?"

With each word of his explanation, my blood boiled hotter. Evidently, Voodoo had a vision of Reya betraying us. After that, Venom had Facet monitoring her phone and laptop. He found out Reya had overheard us saying that Luis was Laila's father, and after we kicked her out, she found a way to reach him. She offered him Laila's whereabouts for a big chunk of money.

"You're sure he's dead?" I asked. Not because I doubted them, but because I was hoping I could send him to hell myself.

"Positive."

"What about Reya?" My teeth were grinding.

"No sign of her. Facet says it's like she vanished. So either Luis killed her or she took the money, got a new identity, and ran. My money is on Luis. I can't see him giving up a bunch of cash. Especially to some bitch that had been kicked out of the MC because she couldn't be trusted. If she'd turn on us for a dime, she'd turn on him. Nope, he probably got the info, then made her disappear."

What a shitshow.

"Fuck," I muttered, and that word held more emotion than I cared to admit. The thought of something happening to Laila at this point in our lives, when we'd finally found each other again, ripped my soul to shreds. I owed Blade and Squirrel a debt of gratitude.

"Like I said, she's fine. I got her calmed down, and she's sleeping soundly. Cookie has checked on her a few times."

"Jesus, don't have Cookie checking on her. Have Willow do it," I said as I pulled the hairband out and ran a frustrated hand through my tangled hair. Though Laila said she didn't have a problem with Cookie, I knew there was still some jealousy.

"Yes, boss," he said snidely. Immediately, I was chagrined.

"Sorry, Pres. Please have Willow check on her instead of Cookie."

He chuckled. "I'm just fucking with you. Okay, I've been up all damn night, and I want to hold my woman before Kristin wakes up. Let your woman sleep. I'll have her call you when she gets up."

His baby girl was beautiful, but they'd been having a hard time keeping her on a schedule. Thankfully, Venom's gram lived in a little guest house behind theirs, so she helped out a lot.

"Thanks, bro."

"That's what family is for," he said before he hung up.

I might as well not have lain down, because I didn't really sleep much. Before I knew it, Phoenix's alarm was going off, and we were getting ready to head to the airport.

Eliska was waiting with a small bag at a table in the corner when we entered the common area. Despite her ordeal, she seemed prim and proper as she sat with her hands folded, staring at them. Creed, Reaper, and a prospect sat at their bar.

"She insists she's going back with you guys," Creed said, motioning his head to the woman over his shoulder. "We offered to let her get her bearings back and stay here for a bit, but she said no."

After we found out she didn't have a brother, she refused to meet whoever it was that said he was. Poor girl was going to have trust issues from hell after all this, and I didn't blame her one bit. I also couldn't fault her for not wanting to stay there.

Hawk nodded. "I understand. Let me call the airline to see if I can get her a seat. We'll keep her safe and out of the way while we find out who this guy is that claimed to be her brother."

Creed shook all of our hands.

"Thank you for everything, Creed," Hawk said as he held Creed's hand in a firm grip.

"It's what brothers do," he said with a hint of a grin.

Hawk went over to talk to Eliska. Once he confirmed her decision, we settled our travel plans. It was decided that Phoenix and Angel would fly to Iowa with Eliska and take her to the clubhouse. Hawk and I were catching the original flight to Nashville, and we would go to the diner to see who the fuck the dude was claiming to be her brother. Then we'd hop a later flight back to Des Moines.

Asses dragging, we all loaded up in the SUV, and the Jacksonville chapter's prospect drove us to the airport. We thanked him and headed to the security checkpoint.

"Just act natural," I told Eliska. "The IDs are in your real name, and they're good. No one will question a thing."

She nodded and clutched the small tote bag close to her chest. I cast a glance at Hawk, who quickly stepped up and rested a hand on her forearm.

"Everything's going to be just fine. Relax," he said, and she visibly did as he said.

As we made our way through the airport, Eliska stopped me. We all paused, and she scanned the group. "Thank you. It doesn't seem sufficient, but my gratitude is beyond words."

We nodded. Though we took the law into our hands, that was exactly why we did it. For people like her that would've been lost in an overloaded system and the maze of red tape that accompanied that flawed system.

Then they went to their terminal while Hawk and I found ours.

Before we knew it, we were taking our seats and anxiously awaiting takeoff.

By the time we landed in Nashville, it was late afternoon, and we were exhausted. Though we ended up being gone less than two days, it seemed forever.

Hawk and I hopped an Uber and had him drop us off before the diner. We walked up the last block. When we got there, we paused at the corner of the building to glance in through the plate-glass window. You could've blown me over with a feather when I saw the man seated back at the corner table we'd instructed him to be waiting in.

I exchanged a confused glance with Hawk, and we entered the restaurant. The dark-haired man looked up, and a shocked expression painted his face. He stood when we stopped at the table.

"Calix?" Hawk asked. "What the fuck?"

"I'm meeting someone here," he replied as his eyes narrowed. Calix had gone to one of our chapters in Tennessee after helping to save Voodoo. We hadn't seen him since.

"Yeah. Us," I clarified.

"It was you guys? But how? I've been dealing with a woman. I—never mind." He trailed off. "Where is she?" he questioned as his gaze darted around.

"Eliska?" I cocked a brow as I waited for his answer. He nodded.

"Why did you lie about her being your sister?" Hawk demanded.

Calix scanned the room again. "Can we sit?"

Without answering, we all grabbed a chair. Calix propped his forearms on the edge of the table and laced his fingers. Then he stared at them a moment before raising his odd-colored eyes to where we were still waiting for an answer.

"I thought if the person I hired thought she was my sister it would gain more attention, sympathy, empathy? Whatever. Not that I'm sure hackers have any of that, but my contact said she was a woman and was better than she realized. Eliska is actually a good friend. She's a fucking librarian." He sighed when the waitress stopped at our table.

We all ordered coffee.

"Continue," I encouraged him.

"She used to let me into the library after hours to use the internet. We became friends."

"How good of friends?" The vision of what I'd found in that room made my stomach bottom out at telling him what she'd likely endured.

"Not like that. Really, we were simply friends. I didn't lie that she met a guy. They met online, and she flew down to Florida to meet him for the first time. I didn't like it. He seemed too perfect. I wanted to go with her. Of course, that didn't go over well." He huffed.

"I made her promise to call me every day. She told the guy I was her brother and I was worried about her. The first couple of days seemed like she was right. She told me he spoiled the hell out of her. Then she didn't call, so I called her. He gave me some excuse. Same thing the next day. So I tried again later that day. Conveniently, she was always away from her phone. Something seemed incredibly off, so I looked into him. He was some car salesman at a small lot. No way he made the kind of money he was blowing on her. That's when I found Scarlett through a friend." He raked a hand through his dark hair, then picked up his cup but grimaced when he took a sip.

"What? Can't actually drink anything other than blood?" I teased.

He rolled his eyes and snorted. "I can eat or drink anything I please, but that tastes like shit."

My eyes narrowed on him, because I knew damn well he was a vampire. I lifted my cup and took a drink. "Oh, damn!" It tasted like burned sludge.

Calix smirked. "Told you. Not everything you've read about us is true."

"Hmpf!" I crossed my arms.

"Now where is Eliska?" Calix asked as he leaned toward us.

"She decided to fly back to Iowa, and nothing we said could change her mind. We have another flight to catch," Hawk told him as he pulled some cash out and dropped it on the table.

I reached for my pocket, but Hawk shook his head. "That's plenty for three shitty cups of coffee and a decent tip."

"I don't understand why she didn't know it would be me since we pretended I was her brother already," Calix murmured with a worried frown.

"She'd been through a lot, and trust is likely nonexistent with her at this point. I doubt she thought about it," Hawk explained with a sigh.

"I have a car. If you trust me, I can drive us to the airport," Calix offered with a raised brow.

"Us to the airport?" I asked with a cocked brow.

"If you think I'm not going to see that Eliska is safe with my own two eyes, you're out of your mind," Calix insisted.

My gaze darted outside to the sunny day, then back to our old friend. He chuckled, pulled out a ball cap, and plopped it on his head. "Like I said, don't believe everything you've heard."

We followed him out to a Range Rover with dark-tinted

windows. He hit the key fob and went around to the driver side. Hawk climbed in the front seat, and I took the back.

"Nice wheels," I said, wondering how the hell he afforded it. He'd been a prospect with the shitty Bloody Scorpions when we met him. Not because he really wanted to join them, but he was trying to get close to them to find out more about their trafficking connections. He did something with missing kids and shit, if I remembered right.

"Thanks," he replied with a grin.

Calix parked his vehicle in long-term parking, and we went into the airport where he purchased a ticket on our flight. It had to have cost him a small fortune.

Since our layover hadn't been that long, we were boarding in no time. I checked my phone one last time before putting it in airplane mode.

The closer we got to home, the more anxious I became. Laila hadn't called me yet, and I was worried. Surely, she was awake by then. I hoped when we landed that I'd have missed calls or text messages from her.

We caught another Uber from the airport.

Hawk had called ahead, so when we got to the clubhouse the gate was open. I was shocked to see a large section of our fence destroyed and a temporary one in its place. It seemed Venom had left a few details out of the story.

The prospect closed the gate, and we parked out front.

When we went inside, I glanced around for Laila, but she wasn't in the common area.

There was a muffled shout as Eliska covered her mouth with both hands and jumped up from the table she'd been sitting at with Blade. She ran at Calix and threw herself in his arms. He spun her around, and I saw Blade's eyes narrow as his chin moved back and forth in irritation.

I needed to tell him she wasn't a girl for him to be messing with.

"How did you not know it was me?" Calix asked her. I missed his reply because something more important caught my attention.

"Lucian?" I heard softly, and I turned toward the hall to the rooms.

Then Laila was in my arms with her legs wrapped around my waist. I cradled her head against my shoulder as I held her tight.

That was all it took. All was right in the world in that moment.

"We'll be back," I said as I carried her, clinging to me like a spider monkey, back to our room.

The mission might've been successful, but I had some adrenaline I needed to work off.

TWENTY-FOUR

Laila

"BORN AGAIN"—DEADSET SOCIETY

I didn't ask him any questions, because I was too relieved he made it back safe. My nose buried in his neck, I squeezed tighter.

"I was so worried about you," I said against his skin.

"Me? Fuck, Laila. Venom filled me in on what happened. Are you sure you're okay?" he questioned between kisses and nips to my neck and jaw.

"Physically? Yeah. Mentally? I'll get back to you on that," I admitted, then regretted saying anything, because he tried to peel me off him. I fought tooth and nail and held on tight.

"Baby, I don't want to make things worse. Because things were a little… intense. I need it…." He cleared his throat and wouldn't meet my gaze. Completely on the same page after everything that had happened, I gripped his face.

"What? You need it rough? Because I hope that's what you

mean. Every minute since the shit that went down with Luis, I've been numb. I need to feel. Please make me feel," I begged.

If I thought there was going to be a mad destruction of our clothing coupled with crazy hot sex, well, I was wrong.

And right.

Savoring each inch of my skin he revealed, Ghost seductively removed my shirt, then leaned down to suck my nipple through the lace of my bra. He dropped to his knees, and his rough hands wrapped around my waist to then slip up my back to hold me captive as his tongue and mouth continued the process of soaking my panties. When the fabric was good and wet, he moved to the other one.

I gasped when the button of my jeans popped open and looked down to see he'd brought one dexterous hand around to unfasten them. Before I knew it, they were pooled around my ankles, along with the wet red lace of my thong.

Two thick fingers filled me, and I damn near wept when he began to slowly slide them in and out with a hooking motion.

My head fell back, and I threaded my fingers into his dark golden hair. A heated sigh escaped me, and I trembled with need as I impatiently tugged on his shirt.

He chuckled into my cleavage but had mercy on me, returning to his feet. "I wanted to worship you and take my time, but you're making it hard," he murmured as he removed his fingers from my dripping and aching slit.

Bold, I grabbed his rock-hard cock through his jeans and squeezed. "I don't want you to take your time, and I want it hard. Hard is good," I panted as I pulled at his T-shirt, and he lifted his arms above his head for me to tug it off. Except I was too short and ended up jumping trying to get it off.

With a smirk, he ducked his head, gripped the back, and did that hot man thing where they tug it off one-handed from the back.

Finally.

My fingers plucked at his belt, and he helped me divest his sexy ass of those pesky jeans.

"Bed," I ordered, pointing.

"Yes, ma'am," he replied with a half smile before he raked his gaze over my naked body and fell back to the mattress.

I nearly giggled at the way his cock bounced when he did. Instead, I crawled up over him like a panther on the prowl. When I straddled his thighs, I wrapped my fingers around his girth and circled my thumb through the slippery precum.

His eyes slammed shut, and he shoved his head back into the pillow. His arms were beautiful as the muscles corded under his golden tan skin.

"You should let me pierce this," I said before I pulled my bottom lip between my teeth until it stopped on the hoop. His eyes opened wide, and his mouth seemed to move but no words came out.

"Fuck. That," he finally said, ending with an inhaled hiss when I leaned down and licked the end of his cock like it was an ice-cream cone melting in the heat. Moaning, I sucked and drew the flat of my tongue around his shaft as he panted.

By the time I couldn't stand it anymore, I released him with a pop and scooted forward to line him up. Two shallow dips, and I fit the head in my heated core. When I dropped my hips to his, he reflexively reached for them, but I stopped him.

Winding our fingers together, palms mirroring each other's, I raised his hands to rest by his head, then leaned forward as I started to grind. His bright blue gaze held mine the entire time, and his teeth were gritted as he let me get myself off with his body.

One last swivel of my hips, and my pussy clenched his cock tightly before it spasmed wildly around him. Riding out the waves, I continued rocking my hips over his. When they slowed to only occasional flutters, he grunted and thrust his hips up at the same time as he said, "Fuck, that's killing me. Enough."

He flipped us, and his lean hips snapped forward, burying that beautiful cock so deep, I saw stars. Then he unleashed the beast I'd seen impatiently waiting in his gaze as I rode him.

I'd wanted rough, and he sure as fuck gave it to me.

Eager, I wrapped my legs around his thighs and hung on.

Powerful strokes left me panting as my breasts bounced with each one. The pounding of my heart was paced with the slapping of our skin. Heated breath skimmed my cheek as he leaned down and kissed my jaw, then bit and sucked on my neck as he dropped to his elbows.

I arched up and turned my head to give him better access. With each thrust I knew I would come again. That familiar tingle and the pressure that rapidly increased told me I was almost there.

His pace became erratic, and I knew he was getting close too. I wanted him to come with me, so I pushed his buttons by talking dirty to him.

"That's it," I breathlessly crooned. "Come in my pussy. Fill me with that hot cum, then fuck me until it's all over my thighs."

"That fucking mouth," he muttered as he buried himself deep in my sheath.

At the first pulse of his thick shaft, my orgasm exploded, and I moaned. Everything seemed to shatter around us—nothing but tiny shards of our bodies flying in every direction.

When I finally drifted down from my high, I realized my nails were buried in his back, and I gently relaxed my hands to soothe the damage.

"Fucking hell, that was hot," he panted before pressing a sloppy kiss to my neck, then capturing my lips in a drawn-out, sloweddown version of what our bodies had done.

For a moment we lay connected, limbs tangled and sweaty skin sliding with each ragged breath we took.

"They're going to wonder where we are," I finally said, breaking the perfect silence in the aftermath of our storm.

He chuckled, and it caused his softening length to slip partway out. I whimpered as my bottom lip stuck out in an exaggerated pout. His teeth nipped it and tugged on the metal ring.

"Come on, then. I want you to meet Calix and Eliska."

When I went to wash up, he stopped me. As I watched our reflection over the sink, my lips parted. His hand plunged between my legs, and he dragged our combined release up my body. Our gazes locked as he rubbed it everywhere he could reach.

"You can shower tonight. Right now, I want to know you're painted with my cum under your clothes—marked as mine," he whispered in my ear as his eyes still held mine in the mirror.

I was speechless and so turned on, I wanted to say fuck meeting his friends and have him bend me over the sink right then and there. Instead, he gave me a knowing grin and left me there. I heard the clink of his belt as he dressed.

"Fucker," I whispered, getting a grip on my body and its need for him.

With playfully narrowed eyes, I dressed. As I pulled my panties back on, I stared at him. Before I pulled them over my hips, I dipped two fingers in my still wet pussy, then sucked on them.

An evil grin lifted the corner of my mouth as his pupils dilated and he seemed to growl. Then I quickly dressed. "Let's go," I said as I grabbed his hand and damn near skipped out of the room.

Introductions were made, and I nearly died when Calix raised my hand to his lips and gave me a sharp glance with a cocked brow.

Ghost, that asshole, busted out laughing. Everyone else eyed us like we had lost our marbles.

Voodoo and Kira were sitting at one end, with their son sleeping on Voodoo's shoulder. It was an utterly ovary-exploding sight. One of their German shepherds lay at their feet, while the other one, Zaka, sat at my feet staring at me and nudging my hand if I stopped petting him.

"I cannot thank you enough for finding me," Eliska said as she gripped my free hand tightly. She was prettier than her pictures had given her credit for. Curly blonde hair framed a heart-shaped face, a slightly upturned button nose, naturally flushed cheeks, and eyes of darkest midnight. I'd never seen blue eyes that reminded me of the ocean at night.

In short, she was ethereal and reminded me of a fairy. And her resilience after what she must've endured was monumental.

I'd assumed Calix and Eliska were siblings until I found out that wasn't the case at all. As we all took seats in the sectional and couches that surrounded the big-screen TV, I watched them in an attempt to figure them out. At first, I thought they were an item, but then I realized his arm around her shoulders on the back of the couch was casual and his smiles and touches were platonic. Though each one had Blade shooting daggers at Calix, which I found odd.

"Well, I hate to break up the party, but we better get on the road, Eliska."

That's when I realized she wasn't completely unfazed by her ordeal. Her gaze dropped to her lap, and she nervously twisted her fingers. "Calix, I'm not going back."

"What?" he blurted, obviously in shock. "But your job. Your friends," he argued.

"Calix, let's be honest. The only friend I really had was you." She took a deep fortifying breath before she exhaled with puffed cheeks. "The thought of enduring all the questions, pitying looks, and whispers behind my back makes me nauseous. They all knew I was going off to meet my dream man. What a joke."

"It won't be like that," Calix tried to counter, but she held up a hand.

"We both know it will be. It's a small town, and everyone is in everyone's business. That's why you needed to use the library after hours—so they wouldn't hound you and stare because you're the 'new guy in town.'"

At that, Angel coughed, and Ghost snorted. Phoenix had a raised brow. Glancing at the guys Ghost called brothers, I realized they all looked like they knew something Eliska and I didn't. Even the ol' ladies that were there seemed fascinated with their nails or invisible threads on their jeans. I made a mental note to grill Ghost later.

"Where are you going to go? At least let me help you get set up somewhere new." Calix tried again.

"Ankeny isn't a bad place. I bet they could use a good librarian," Blade said in a low, gruff voice, surprising us all. Ghost gave him a stare that seemed to hold a warning, as did Hawk, but Blade looked away and ignored them with a shrug. "It was an idea," he mumbled before lifting his beer to his mouth.

"Maybe," Eliska said with her own shrug and cheeks that seemed a bit darker than before. "It's pretty here with all the leaves changing. It reminds me a little of Tennessee."

Hmmm.

"Well, then if Venom and the boys are okay with it, maybe I'll stay here until you figure it out," Calix smoothly murmured as he cast a calculating look at Blade.

Loralei started offering places she knew that might be hiring, and Voodoo's ol' lady, Kira, nodded. "I bet I could get you a job as a receptionist at the vet clinic until you find something. Laila is going to be starting as a tech in training, so you'd have a couple of familiar faces."

Ghost's head whipped to face me. "Oh?"

I gave him a cheesy grin. He knew when I was young I'd always wanted to be a veterinarian, but life had upended those plans. I loved animals, and the idea of working at the clinic excited me. My fingers sifted through Zaka's thick black fur, and he sighed contentedly.

"Next thing you know, we'll have one of those hairy beasts running around the house," Ghost grumbled.

"Well, we have to find a house first." I batted my eyes rapidly.

He dropped his head to the back of the couch with a huff. Everyone laughed.

I leaned over and kissed his shoulder. "Don't worry. I'll always love you most," I teased with an impish grin.

His hand cupped the back of my head, and he pressed his forehead to mine as he gazed into my eyes. "Not as much as I love you," he whispered.

"Show me how much later?" I whispered back.

The corner of his mouth kicked up.

"Absolutely."

EPILOGUE

"**A**re you almost ready?" I called. We were going to be late, and I'd never hear the end of it.

"I'm coming!" Laila called from the bedroom. After I'd returned home from rescuing Calix's friend Eliska, Laila and I had bought a house—In the same fucking neighborhood as Voodoo, Angel, and Chains.

It had been almost a year since we moved in, and we were supposed to be going to a Halloween party at Chains and Jasmine's.

She sauntered out of our room, and I had to adjust my dick. "Goddamn, woman. Are you trying to kill me? You can't be parading around in front of the brothers in that!"

Laila looked like a wet dream in a sexy pirate outfit complete with thigh-high black boots and a jaunty hat. She'd let her hair go back to dark blonde, but she had red streaks in it now, and with her tattoos and piercing, she looked like a badass.

One I really wanted to strip out of that fucking costume.

Hips swinging, she closed in on me until we were a mere

breath apart. Then she looked up at me with those big blue eyes. Despite the height of the heeled boots, she barely came to my nose.

"I just figured I better look sexy while I can."

"What the fuck is that supposed to mean?" I growled with a frown. She'd been really bummed since turning thirty, but I couldn't give a shit. She was beautiful, and she was mine. She'd be the most gorgeous woman in the world to me when she was eighty.

"Well, I doubt if waddling will be overly sexy," she said with a pout. Then she batted her thick lashes as she slid her fingers up my chest to wrap around the back of my neck.

"Huh?"

Slowly, she wet her lower lip, and I was so captivated by the glisten it left behind that I didn't catch the words that she said.

"Are you even listening to me?" She chuckled as I shook my head honestly.

"Sorry, those lips distracted the hell out of me. How about we skip the party and you wrap them around my—" She pressed a finger over my mouth before I could make the suggestion that I thought was a much better idea than attending a Halloween party.

"I'm pregnant," she whispered.

The world stopped spinning. Wind quit blowing; birds were silent. All I could do was blink at her like an idiot. Because I was pretty sure she said she was pregnant.

I pulled my upper body back to look at her flat stomach, not sure what I expected to see, but maybe a suddenly noticeable bump.

"I'm not that far along. I wasn't sure if it was just my irregular periods, so I went to the doctor. I'm about twelve weeks already."

My heart that had stilled with everything around me suddenly exploded and raced until I was nearly dizzy. "You're sure?"

Laughter broke from her lips as she nodded. "Definitely."

She lifted her hat and pulled a paper from it that she handed to me. Eager, I took it and stared. We'd been trying for almost eight months to have a baby because she was paranoid about not being able to have kids before she was too old.

When pregnancy test after test came up negative, we consulted Madame Laveaux on one of her trips. She told us it might not be time and to be patient.

Then she'd pulled me to the side later that night and told me she was worried that because I walked both sides of life and death that maybe I couldn't father children.

"Well?" Her tone trembled slightly.

We'd talked about adopting. We discussed a donor, because I wanted her to experience every aspect of motherhood if she wanted to, but the thought of some other guy's shit in my woman's uterus was not cool.

Call me a dick, because I know a lot of people were okay with that and happy to have a child any way they could; I simply couldn't.

"I'm gonna be a dad," I said, staring at the image that blew my mind. It actually looked like a baby. Arms, legs, kinda big head, little potbelly. It was perfect.

"Yeah," she sighed.

My gaze lifted, and I met her sky-blue one that waited expectantly. "And you're gonna be a mom," I said in awe. Her eyes filled with tears, then she nodded.

A grin split my face, and I scooped her up and swung her around. She held her hat and squealed with laughter until I abruptly stopped and gently set her down.

"Shit, I'm so sorry. Are you okay? Did that hurt you? Or the baby?"

A snicker escaped as she reached up to cradle my face with her soft palm. I clutched her forearm. Then I turned her arm to press a kiss over the little hourglass that was framed by PROPERTY

OF on the top and GHOST on the bottom. It was a reminder that life was short, time passed quickly, and to enjoy every minute.

"I love you, Laila. Can we get married now?" She had been planning our wedding since I proposed on Valentine's Day. The proposal part had been great. The rest of what transpired was par for the course of our club.

She tapped her finger on her pursed lips as she appeared to think. "I suppose."

"You suppose?" I growled as I leaned down and rubbed my short beard all over her cleavage and neck, eliciting a giggle from her.

Suddenly, I heard the scamper of nails on the hardwood floor, and a fluffy black fur ball barreled into my legs. His paws hit my knee, and his tongue lolled out the side of his mouth.

That was when I saw a small lacy red pile in the hall behind Laila. My eyes darted to Dexter, then I folded my lips between my teeth to keep from laughing.

"What?" Laila asked suspiciously as she reached down to scratch behind his ears. Of course, the little shit ate it up.

I shook my head. "Did he already go out?"

She nodded, but her eyes were nearly slits.

Then I looked at Dexter. "Treat?"

His mouth snapped shut, his front paws hit the floor, and he sat still as could be with his little head cocked to the side.

"Well, kennel up, then," I said, and he was off like a shot, damn near knocking the kennel over with the force of his body slamming inside. I chuckled and got one of his special biscuits that Eliska had started making. Once he was happily munching on it, I closed the door and turned to the stunning woman I loved.

"Uh-oh," I mumbled as I saw her nostrils flare and her boots clicked across the floor.

"Dexterrrr!" she shouted as she picked up the red scraps of

her panties. She shook them at me. "This is the eighth pair this week!"

"You wanted him," I said with a chuckle before she tossed the bits of lace at me with a huff. I swore he was so naughty because she went with the name Blade suggested.

She pointed at him, and he had the gall to lay his head on his paws and look up at her through his kennel door with the saddest puppy-dog eyes I'd ever seen.

I hooked an arm around her waist and brought her attention to me.

"I love you."

"I love you too," she grumped, causing me to smile.

"I love our naughty dog," I continued.

"Me too," she said as she tried to hide the twitch of her lips.

"And I'm going to love our baby," I added, then kissed her red lips. "No, that's not true."

Her eyes widened in horror, and I laughed.

"I already do," I clarified, and she melted.

"Me too" was her soft reply. Then she looked me up and down. A frown wrinkled her brow.

"Where's your costume? We need to leave!"

"Right here," I said as I grabbed the white sheet from the couch and dropped it over my head. I'd cut two holes for my eyes. Then I disappeared.

Her face went deadpan as she blinked at the man-shaped sheet that appeared to have nothing under it.

"Really?" she drily questioned.

"I thought it was perfect."

"God help me if this is a boy and he acts like you."

My chuckle made the sheet flutter in front of my mouth. "It'll be worse if it's a girl and she acts like me."

Her eyes bugged. "No! Don't you put that on our child! They

are going to be a saint, they are going to be a saint, they are going to be a saint," she kept mumbling as she grabbed her plastic sword and a small leather purse thing that wrapped around her waist over her sash.

As we went out the door, I laughed because she was still saying it. She poked me with her sword. But I honestly didn't care if our child was naughty or a saint; I'd love him or her until the end of time, just as she would.

Or until all the stars fall from the sky.

THE END.

ACKNOWLEDGEMENTS

If you're actually reading this, holy cow—you're dedicated. I thank *you* first and foremost! KISSES! Okay, batten down the hatches and hang on, this is gonna be a little long.

This book is dedicated to my daughter, Rhiannon. I know you might be thinking, "What? She already dedicated a book to her." What you may not know is you almost didn't get Ghost's story or any other story after him. You see, I was drowning—literally— and she saved me. How do you truly thank someone for saving your life? You can't, because there will never be enough gratitude. That experience made me look at a lot of things differently. Yes, I still struggle with the anxiety if I think about it too much. I still see the churning, dark water that was swallowing me, every time I close my eyes. Yet here I am… writing this long ass thank you to everyone who made this possible. So yeah, my daughter is my hero. I love you, Rhiannon.

Thank you to all of you who keep reading my words. You're the ones giving me a reason to write and hit "publish."

Some of this will be repetitive (if you read all this mumbo-jumbo) because all of you are always in my corner and I love you to pieces.

PSH, my very own Porn Star Hubby (if you ever meet me, ask me to tell you the story). Thank you for being my book pimp. Hahaha! Sometimes I think you sell my books better than I can. :P Thank you for loading, unloading, carting books, banners, and swag from here to there and everywhere in-between. I love you bunches.

Thank you to **Pam, Kristin, Brenda, Lisa** for being my betas and letting me bounce ideas off you at all hours of the night. I seriously couldn't do this without you. YOU ARE MY SQUAD!

Shout out to **Kristine's Street Team**! Y'all mother-freaking rock! You ladies continually go above and beyond for me and my books. Never in a million years could I thank you enough. Hugs and kisses!

Olivia, you're the bomb-diggity of editors; the absolute best. You've ruined reading for me at times, but I love you bunches! Thank you for fixing all my oopsies, calling me on the stuff that doesn't make sense, questioning my wording, and for fixing all those pesky commas that I hate. It's your touch that polishes my book babies until they shine.

Penny. Where do I start? My beautiful forever friend. Thank you for always believing in me, even when I didn't believe in myself. <3 Every time I tell you how good things are going and you tell me you're not surprised, I want to cry. Your faith in me is eternally humbling. You can see the light at the end of the dark tunnel that is nursing school—you've got this!

Lisa and **Brenda**, y'all are the best and I cannot thank you enough for your support, advice, and friendship. And wine. To think it all started with a lunch born from the love of books. 2020 Book Signing events may have went to shit, but we're still doing our thing! Always with wine.

Lucian Bane, you did an amazing job on this cover! It turned out exactly the way I envisioned it.

Wander Aguiar, this image of Alex is absolutely captivating. **Alex**'s stunning image made this cover one of my favorites. Thank you.

Stacey of **Champagne Book Designs**, never, ever, ever forget—you are a goddess. Every single time, you make each page beautiful. I can't say whether the print or digital are my favorite because I love them all so much. Thanks bunches, and guess what's almost here? Shameless! It still hasn't set in that I will be there as an AUTHOR! Can you believe it? Craziness!

Ladies of **Kristine's Krazy Fangirls**, every one of you are the bomb-diggity. You're my personal little cheerleading team and I love you all! (((BIG HUGS)))! I thank you for your comments, your support, and your love of all things books. Come join us if you're not part of the group www.facebook.com/groups/kristineskrazyfangirls

My last, but never least, is a massive thank you to America's servicemen and women who protect our freedom on a daily basis. They do their duty, leaving their families for weeks, months, and years at a time, without asking for praise or thanks. I would also like to remind the readers that not all combat injuries are visible, nor do they heal easily. These silent, wicked injuries wreak havoc on their minds and hearts while we go about our days completely oblivious. Thank you all for your service.

OTHER BOOKS BY
KRISTINE ALLEN

Demented Sons MC Series - Iowa
Colton's Salvation
Mason's Resolution
Erik's Absolution
Kayde's Temptation

Straight Wicked Series
Make Music With Me
Snare My Heart
No Treble Allowed
String Me Up

Demented Sons MC Series - Texas
Lock and Load
Styx and Stones
Smoke and Mirrors
Jax and Jokers
Got Your Six
(Formerly in Remember Ryan Anthology - Coming Soon!)

RBMC - Ankeny Iowa
Voodoo
Angel
A Very Venom Christmas
Chains
Haunting Ghost
Blade (Coming Soon!)
Sabre (Coming Soon!)

The Iced Series
Hooking
Tripping
Roughing
Holding (Coming Soon!)

Heels, Rhymes, & Nursery Crimes
Roses Are Red (RBMC connection)
Violets Are Blue (Coming Soon!)

Twisted Steel Anthology II
Snow's Addiction (DSMC Iowa President)

Pinched and Cuffed Anthology
The Weight of Honor (Coming Soon!)

ABOUT THE AUTHOR

Kristine Allen lives in beautiful Central Texas with her adoring husband. They have four brilliant, wacky, and wonderful children. She is surrounded by twenty-six acres, where her five horses, five dogs, and six cats run the place. She's a hockey addict and feeds that addiction with season tickets to the Texas Stars. Kristine realized her dream of becoming a contemporary romance author after years of reading books like they were going out of style and having her own stories running rampant through her head. She works as a night shift nurse, but in stolen moments, taps out ideas and storylines until they culminate in characters and plots that pull her readers in and keep them entranced for hours.

Reviews are the life blood of an indie author. If you enjoyed this story, please consider leaving a review on the sales channel of your choice, bookbub.com, goodreads.com, allauthor.com, or your review platform of choice, to share your experience with other interested readers. Thank you! <3

Follow Kristine on:

Facebook: www.facebook.com/kristineallenauthor

Instagram: www.instagram.com/_jessica_is_kristine.allen_

Twitter @KAllenAuthor

TikTok: vm.tiktok.com/ZMebdkNpS

All Author: www.kristineallen.allauthor.com

BookBub: www.bookbub.com/authors/kristine-allen

Goodreads: www.goodreads.com/kristineallenauthor

Webpage:www.kristineallenauthor.com

Made in the USA
Columbia, SC
20 January 2025

52150556R00133